D0590896

TALES OF BRAVE ADVENTURE

First published in 1963
Reprinted in 1984

Published by Deans International Publishing
52–54 Southwark Street, London SE1 1UA
A Division of The Hamlyn Publishing Group Limited
London · New York · Sydney · Toronto

Copyright © Darrell Waters Limited 1963

ISBN 0 603 03257 5

Printed and bound by Purnell and Sons (Book Production) Ltd.,
Paulton, Bristol.
Member of BPCC plc

TALES OF BRAVE ADVENTURE

RETOLD BY
ENID BLYTON

DEANS
INTERNATIONAL
PUBLISHING

CONTENTS

	PAGE
HOW ROBIN HOOD BECAME AN OUTLAW . . .	7
HOW ROBIN HOOD MET LITTLE JOHN . . .	10
HOW ROBIN HOOD TURNED BUTCHER . . .	15
HOW ROBIN HOOD MET WILL SCARLET . . .	24
THE WEDDING OF ALLEN-A-DALE	30
ROBIN HOOD AND THE BISHOP	36
HOW THE BISHOP HUNTED ROBIN HOOD . . .	42
ROBIN HOOD AND MAID MARIAN	52
THE GOLDEN ARROW	57
THE SHOOTING-MATCH	62
ROBIN HOOD AND THE TINKER OF BANBURY . .	69
HOW KING RICHARD CAME TO THE GREENWOOD .	75
THE DEATH OF ROBIN HOOD	87
THE ENCHANTED SWORD	96
THE ROUND TABLE	102
THE FINDING OF THE SWORD EXCALIBUR . .	104
BALIN, THE KNIGHT OF THE TWO SWORDS . .	108
PRINCE GERAINT AND THE SPARROWHAWK . .	115
THE FURTHER ADVENTURES OF GERAINT AND ENID .	122
GARETH, THE KNIGHT OF THE KITCHEN . . .	132
SIR GARETH GOES ADVENTURING . . .	138
THE BOLD SIR PEREDUR	148
THE QUEST OF THE HOLY GRAIL . . .	154
THE ADVENTURES OF SIR GALAHAD . . .	158
SIR MORDRED'S PLOT	166
SIR GAWAINE MEETS SIR LANCELOT . . .	172
THE PASSING OF ARTHUR	178

How Robin Hood Became An Outlaw

ROBIN was a strong and handsome youth, skilful with his bow and quick with his fists. He lived happily in his father's house, merry and glad the whole year round. His two great friends were Will, his cousin, and Maid Marian,

Very happy were they in the Greenwood.

and very happy were they when they played together in the Greenwood they all loved.

Then one day enemies came to attack Robin's father. In vain did his men, led by Robin, try to repulse the foe. The old man was killed, and his house was set on fire. All his men were slain, and none escaped save only Robin. He owed his life to his trusty bow, for so well did he shoot that the enemy did not dare to come near him.

Robin watched his home flaming to the sky, and then, full of grief for his father, he ran weeping to Sherwood Forest, carrying only his bow and arrows with him. He rushed through the trees, deeper and deeper into the wood. Then

He vowed he would revenge himself.

at last, tired out, he flung himself down and thought bitterly of all that had happened that day.

He had nothing left. His home was gone, his father lay dead, his men were killed, his land taken from him. Anger came into his heart, and he vowed he would revenge himself. He would live in the Greenwood, and become an outlaw. Rich men and greedy priests he would rob, and their money he would give to the poor who had no one to help them.

His home should be the forest, and his men outlaws like himself. He would feed on the King's deer and lead a merry life under the trees.

Thus began the adventures of Robin Hood. Not very long was he alone, for as soon as men heard that brave Robin was an outlaw, they went to join him, and became his Merry Men. At first he was sad, for he grieved for his lost home, and missed his two friends, Maid Marian and Will. But in a short time he grew to love his adventurous life, and his laughter rang out as loudly as the others.

His men wore suits of Lincoln green, with hoods over their heads. Some say that Robin took his name from these, and was called Robin i' the Hood, soon shortened to Robin Hood, and that may quite well be so. He loved his men with all his heart, and they would have followed him to the ends of the earth.

There was Little John, Robin's chief man, a strong fellow seven feet high, Will Scarlet, Allen-a-Dale, Much the Miller's son, fat Friar Tuck, Will Stutely, George-a-Green, Arthur-a-Bland, the sturdy tanner of Nottingham, Gilbert of the White Hand, and many another.

Merry was the life they led under the Greenwood Tree, and many were their adventures. They were all outlaws, but the common people loved them, for Robin Hood did them no harm but only good. He had sworn an oath, and kept it to his dying day. This is the oath he swore:

> "I swear to honour God and the King,
> To help the weak and fight the strong,
> To take from the rich and give to the poor,
> So God will help me with His power."

How Robin Hood Met Little John

ONE MORNING Robin Hood took his bow and arrows, and set out to seek adventure. The day was sunny and fair, and Robin's heart was gay.

"I go walking through the forest," he said to his men. "Keep within sound of my horn."

Off he went, and walked gaily till he came to the edge of the forest. He set off down the highway, and came to a brook, which had a log bridge across it. Robin saw that a puddle lay at his end, so he took a leap over it, and landed on the bridge.

Then he saw someone crossing from the other side, a great giant of a fellow, seven feet high, carrying in his hand a stout young sapling for a stick. Robin hurried to the middle, trying to cross first, and the stranger did the same.

They met in the middle, and neither would give way an inch.

"Go back, fellow, whilst I cross!" commanded Robin, who was used to being obeyed by all his men.

The huge fellow laughed.

"Ho!" he said mockingly; "I give way only to a better man than myself!"

"I'll push you into the stream!" cried Robin in a rage. "Go back, I say, before harm comes to you."

The big man did not move.

"Pitch me in, then!" he said. "You will do it easily if you are a better man than I!"

"Wait here whilst I cut myself a cudgel like yours!" cried Robin, eager for a fight.

He leapt to the bank, and soon cut a stout oak staff with his hunting-knife. The big man stood still in the midst of the

The fight went on for half an hour.

bridge whilst he fetched it, and swung his great staff easily in his hands.

"Are you ready?" cried Robin, leaping back to the middle of the bridge, and flourishing his staff round his head. "One, two——"

"*Three!*" shouted the other, and struck at Robin with his stick. He swerved aside, and smote at the giant hard. Whack! But the big fellow struck Robin back, and almost sent him into the river.

The fight went on for half an hour. Each smote the other, and gave some hard blows. The giant was strong, but Robin was quick, and neither would budge an inch from the bridge. Whack, bang, went the two stout sticks, and many blows fell on arms and shoulders, making the two fighters dance with pain. But neither of them would cry "Enough!"

For some time the giant grinned broadly, but when Robin got in a very sharp stroke his face became red and full of anger. He snorted, and stepped forward to give Robin a furious blow, but that nimble fellow dodged the stroke, and coming back at the giant, he dealt him such a buffet that the stranger reeled and nearly lost his footing.

He struck at Robin as he staggered back, and caught him by surprise. Robin had looked to see the giant fall into the water, but even as he watched, the stick came down on his head with a resounding whack.

Down he fell into the water with a fine splash, and, half dazed, groped for the bank. The big giant roared heartily to see him fall, but when he saw that he was half stunned, he quickly ran across the bridge, gave his brawny hand to Robin, and pulled him forth from the water.

Robin sat down on the grass and gasped. Then he rubbed his head where the stick had caught him.

"By my life," he said, "you hit full well!"

Then he took his horn, and blew upon it. At once there

came answering shouts, and out from the forest behind ran
a round dozen of Robin's Merry Men. When they saw their
master on the ground, wet through, they were astonished.

"What has happened, Master?" cried Will Stutely. "There
is not a dry stitch on your body!"

"This fellow would not let me cross the bridge," said
Robin, with a twinkle in his eye. "I tickled him in the ribs

Swung him right into the water.

with my stick, and he patted me on the head, so that I fell
into the stream."

"Ho, give him a taste of his own porridge!" cried Will.
"Come on, lads!"

They seized the giant, and holding him so that he could
not move even a finger, they carried him to the stream. Then
with a "one, two, three!" they swung him right into the
water, where he disappeared with a mighty splash.

In a trice the big fellow was out of the brook, and knocked
Will Stutely down, and three others too. Then all the rest

of the men threw themselves on him, and kept him down, though it was as much as they could do, for he heaved himself about, and cried out that he would fight them all, three at a time, if they would let him.

"Let him be!" said Robin. "He is the goodliest man I have ever seen, and I will fight no more with him."

"Tell me your name," demanded the giant, "for I like you well."

"I am known as Robin Hood, and these are my Merry Men," said Robin.

"By all the saints!" cried the giant in surprise. "Then I would I had not beaten you, for I came hither to ask to join your company. But now I am afraid that you will bear me ill-will for having pitched you into the stream."

"Nay!" said Robin, with a laugh. "Never would I bear ill-will for that! And did not you get pitched in too? Clasp hands with me, and tell me your name."

"Men call me John Little," said the giant, taking Robin's hand with joy.

"Enter our company, John Little," said Robin. "You are welcome. Give us your whole body, mind, and heart until death."

"They are yours," said John.

"Ho!" said Will Stutely; "let us christen this little stranger."

He filled his horn with water, and splashed it over John.

"I give you a new name, little man!" he cried. "You shall be called, not John Little, but Little John!"

When the men heard this name being given to the giant, they roared with laughter; Robin laughed too, and Little John joined him. Then off they went to feast in the forest, and Robin was glad at heart, for he knew he had that day made a faithful friend, who would be loyal to him all his life through.

How Robin Hood Turned Butcher

ROBIN HOOD often went into Nottingham, which was bold of him, for there was a price set upon his head. The Sheriff was his bitter enemy, and would willingly have given half his wealth to have the defiant outlaw safely under lock and key. His soldiers were always on the look-out for Robin, and for this reason he used to disguise himself when he wished to enter the town.

Now it came to Robin's ears that the Sheriff had grumbled at his soldiers for not capturing him before now.

" If I could only see the rascal face to face, if I could only have him within my reach, then should you see how I would deal with him ! " shouted the angry Sheriff.

When Robin heard what he had said, he smiled broadly.

" By my life," he cried, " I have a mind to grant the Sheriff his wish ! He shall see me face to face ! "

So off he set to go to Nottingham. On the way there he met a fat butcher on a horse, taking with him a load of meat to sell at the Fair in the town.

" Hail, friend ! " said Robin. " Where do you go with your meat ? "

" Good-day to you," said the butcher. " I am a simple butcher, and I go to Nottingham my flesh to sell. Who are you ? "

" I am Robin Hood," was the answer, and the fat butcher nearly fell off his horse in terror.

" Do not treat me ill ! " he cried. " I speak truth when I say that I am but a poor butcher."

" Have no fear," answered Robin. " I would never rob a

poor man, I promise you. But I would make a bargain with you, butcher."

"Speak on," said the trembling man.

"I would be a butcher this day, and sell meat in the town," said Robin. "Will you sell me your mare, your meat, and your dress for four marks?"

"That will I!" cried the butcher in joy. He jumped down, and gave Robin his blouse and his apron, in return for which Robin handed him his suit of Lincoln Green. Then, with the four marks safely in his purse, the butcher went merrily back home, whilst Robin set the mare's head to Nottingham, and rode whistling on his way.

He went to the market-place, where all the other butchers stood, and set out his wares. He had no idea how to sell meat, and he cried it so cheaply that every one came to his stall to buy. The other butchers, who could not afford to sell so cheaply, stood near by, scowling at the merry fellow who sang and whistled as he sold his meat.

"He is a foolish youth who has sold his father's lands, and taken up trading," said one butcher.

"He is a robber who has murdered a butcher and taken his horse and his meat," said another. But Robin only laughed at them, and went on selling his meat to the people who crowded round him.

Then an old butcher came up to him, and spoke.

"If you are a butcher, you must join our Guild, and learn the rules of our trade," he said. "We dine at the Sheriff's house to-day, and you must join us."

Robin asked nothing better, and he quickly agreed, smiling to think that the Sheriff would soon have his wish granted—he would see Robin face to face!

When the time came, he went with the other butchers to the Sheriff's mansion. The Sheriff was seated at the head of the table, and he greeted the butchers pompously. They set

He cried his wares so cheaply that every one came.

Robin at his right hand, for they had whispered to the Sheriff that he might be a rich young man, and easily robbed of his goods.

So the Sheriff made much of Robin, and jested with him gaily. Robin cracked many jokes, and kept the Sheriff and all

" Now, my fine fellows, be merry this day ! "

the company in fits of laughter, but little did any of them guess that he was the bold Robin Hood.

When the servants set out the meat and drink, Robin stood up.

" Now, my fine fellows, be merry this day, for I will pay the bill ! " he cried. " Spare not the meat and the wine, but have your fill ! "

" Hear, hear ! " cried all the company.

"Now you are a right good fellow!" said the Sheriff.
"But you cannot pay to-day, for I give the feast. You must
have much land and many a head of hornèd beasts to spend
your money so freely."

"You say true," said Robin, twinkling at the Sheriff. "I
have five hundred hornèd beasts, and cannot sell one. That is
why I have turned butcher, good Sheriff. But I like not the
trade overmuch, and gladly would I sell the whole herd
cheaply if I could but find a buyer."

The Sheriff pricked up his ears. Five hundred beasts to be
sold cheaply! What fool was this? Ho, the Sheriff would do
the buying!

"Five hundred beasts, say you?" he said to Robin.

"Yes, five hundred and ten," said Robin. "I would sell
them for twenty pounds—or do you think that is too dear?"

The Sheriff could hardly believe his ears.

"Nay, good fellow," he said; "I will buy them from you,
for I love to help any man in my shire."

"Oh, sir," said Robin, pretending to be overcome with
joy and gratitude; "this is indeed good of you. You are kind
and generous beyond belief. Never will you regret your
kindness, I promise you."

"Well, drive your herd into the market-place to-morrow,"
said the Sheriff, "and I will pay you."

"I cannot easily do that," said Robin, "for they are much
scattered. But they are not far from here. Will you not come
with me to-morrow, and choose your own beasts from my
great herd?"

"That will I!" cried the Sheriff in delight. "You shall stay
here in my house to-night, and on the morrow we will ride
out together."

So Robin Hood slept in the Sheriff's house that night in a
fine bed, and was much honoured. Then when morning came
he and the Sheriff set out together on horseback.

Robin led the way towards Sherwood Forest, and the two soon rode between the trees. The woods were very silent, and the Sheriff began to feel uneasy, though Robin sang and whistled merrily.

"Why do you sing so gaily?" asked the Sheriff.

"To keep my courage up," answered Robin.

"Do you need to fear anything when the Sheriff of Nottingham rides at your side?" asked the Sheriff.

"I fear Robin Hood," said wicked Robin. "They say that that bold outlaw cares little for the Sheriff."

"Do not believe that," said the Sheriff. "He and his men are in mortal fear of me, and they know that their lives are not worth a penny if I set eyes on them."

"But suppose Robin was peering at us from behind some tree now," said Robin, "with all his Merry Men beside him. Would you not be afraid, Sheriff?"

The Sheriff turned pale, and began to tremble. He looked round nervously, and started at every rustle.

"I tell you Robin Hood is too afraid of me to come near my presence," said the Sheriff in a shaking voice. "Besides, he would not dare to come so near the highway as this."

"I saw him here yesterday," said Robin.

"Here!" cried the Sheriff, clutching tightly at his reins in fear.

"Yes, here," said Robin. "He wanted to buy this mare I ride, and this suit I wear, for he said he wished to turn butcher."

Just then a big herd of the King's deer came in sight, and Robin pointed to them.

"There are some of my hornèd cattle, Master Sheriff. Do you not think they are fat? Would you like to buy them, as you promised?"

The Sheriff reined in his horse, and turned his pale face to Robin.

"I did not come to look at herds like these," he said. "Nor did I come to parley with such as you, whoever you may be. I go back to Nottingham, and I bid you take your own way through the forest, ere I hale you before my soldiers."

"Not so fast, Master Sheriff," said Robin, laughing, and he caught the Sheriff's bridle and held it. "I have taken much trouble to bring you here, and I do not wish you to go so soon. You must meet my friends, and dine with me. I will set a good meal before you in return for the one you gave me yesterday."

Robin raised his horn and blew it loudly three times. Away went the frightened deer, and out from the trees came scores of men in Lincoln green, with bows in their hands and swords at their sides. They ran to Robin and bowed to him. The Sheriff watched in amazement, too astonished to try to escape.

"I bring you the Sheriff," said Robin, with a laugh.

"Welcome!" cried the men, bowing in mockery.

"Take the Sheriff's bridle, Little John," commanded Robin Hood, "and lead his horse."

Little John obeyed. Then all the men turned and made their way into the forest. The Sheriff tried to remember the twists and turns of the way, but there were so many that he could not. At last Little John led his horse into a wide space surrounded by great oak trees. A big fire was roasting two of the King's deer, and a most delicious smell arose. Round the fire were more of Robin's men, and they ran to their leader joyfully.

"Ho, good fellows," said Robin, gaily, "prepare a feast to do our guest honour, for seldom do we have such a high visitor!"

The Sheriff was made to sit down on the grass, and a delicious meal was set before him. At first he refused to eat, but Robin Hood commanded him to set to, and, afraid of the merry, mocking outlaw, he obeyed. He could not help enjoying the food, so excellently was it cooked, and so well was it served.

When the meal was over, the Sheriff rose to his feet.

"Thank you for your entertainment," he said. "The evening draws near, and I must go my way to Nottingham. Bid one of your men guide me to the highway, Robin Hood."

There were but forty golden pieces.

"Willingly," said Robin. "But have you not forgotten two things?"

"What are they?" asked the Sheriff, growing pale.

"You came to buy a herd of hornèd beasts," said Robin. "And you have had dinner at the Greenwood Inn, for which you must pay."

"I have only a little money with me," said the frightened Sheriff.

"What sum have you?" asked Robin.

"Forty pieces of gold," said the Sheriff, trembling.

"Count it for me, Little John," commanded Robin.

Little John did so, and it was seen that the Sheriff had spoken the truth, for when his wallet was emptied there were but forty golden pieces in it.

"Well, Sheriff," said Robin, with a laugh, "you have not brought enough to buy the hornèd beasts, so those you must leave with us, and we will not charge you for them. But for your right good dinner you must pay us twenty gold pieces, and also you must swear never to molest us men of the Greenwood."

"I swear by St. George of England never to molest the outlaws in Sherwood Forest!" said the Sheriff. But to himself he thought: "I will not molest them *in* the forest—but ha!—if I catch them *out* of Sherwood, that will be a different tale!"

Little John took twenty gold pieces, and put the rest back into the Sheriff's wallet.

"I myself will guide you back to the highway," said Robin. He took the Sheriff's bridle, and led the horse through the trees until they came out once again on the road to Nottingham.

"Fare you well, Master Sheriff," said Robin Hood. "And the next time you would seek to rob a poor fool of his herds, remember how you wanted to buy *my* hornèd beasts!"

Then he gave the horse a blow on its haunches, and off it trotted down the highway to Nottingham, bearing on its back a sadder and wiser Sheriff.

How Robin Hood Met Will Scarlet

ROBIN HOOD and Little John went walking one fine morning. It was a very hot day, and everywhere was dusty. They went to the little brook where they had first met, and tried to cool themselves by laying hands and face. Then they lay down on the grass in the shade, looking up at the blue sky in great content.

" That sounds a merry bird ! "

As they lay there in silence, they heard the sound of some-one whistling merrily. Then the whistling ceased, and a gay voice began to sing a roundelay.

"That sounds a merry bird!" said Robin, sitting up to listen. "Let us keep silence, Little John; maybe the singer's purse will not be so light as his heart."

Presently, whistling loudly, there came up a strange youth, dressed all in scarlet. His doublet was scarlet, and so was his silken hose. In his scarlet cap was a fine cock feather, and by his side hung a beautiful sword. His long yellow hair curled about his shoulders, and he was indeed good to look upon, though more like a girl in his mincing steps than a man.

"In truth a gay bird!" whispered Little John. "But, Master, he is well built and strong, for all his prettiness. Have a care lest he uses his sword to good purpose!"

"He is but a ladies' man!" answered Robin scornfully. "I lay you my long bow that he will run a mile at the sight of my stout stick! Stay behind this bush, and watch the sport I make with this droll fellow!"

Robin suddenly stepped out from the bushes, and walked in the stranger's path. But the youth paid no heed to him, nor did he even look at him. He walked onwards, as if he would overrun Robin.

"Stop!" cried Robin. "Do you not see that I stand in your way, fellow?"

"But wherefore should I stop?" asked the stranger, looking at Robin for the first time, in seeming surprise.

"Because I bid you," answered Robin.

"And who are you, good fellow?" asked the stranger mockingly.

"That is no matter," said Robin. "But I will tell you this: I am a tax-gatherer, and look to see if travellers have too much in their purses. If they have, I lighten them, and give to those who have less than the just amount. Therefore, pretty youth, give me your purse, and I will see if it weighs too heavy."

The other laughed.

"You are a fine jester," he said. "Pray go on with your jokes, for I am in no hurry, and will stay to hear any further jesting."

"I shall say no more," said Robin, growing angry. "Hand me over your purse."

"You are truly a droll fellow," said the stranger pleasantly. "But I do not hand my purse to every rough lout that demands it. So stand aside, and let me pass."

He began to hum a merry song again, and Robin grew red with rage.

"Hold!" he cried in anger, for he knew that Little John was chuckling in the bushes. "Do as I command, or I will give you a taste of my stick."

"Dear, dear!" said the other, pretending to sigh dolefully. "What a pest the fellow is! Now I shall have to use my sword on him! Shame it is to spoil such a lovely morning!"

He drew his sword, and brandished it before Robin.

"I shall break that pretty weapon of yours with one blow of my oak stick," said Robin. "Put it by, and get yourself a staff like mine from the hedges."

The stranger obeyed. He went to an oak thicket, found a stout sapling, and with one heave pulled it up by the roots. Little John laughed when he saw that, for he knew that Robin would have to put up a fine fight to match the strength shown by the scarlet stranger.

Robin waited till the other had trimmed his stick, and then the two began to fight. Each was surprised at the strength of the other. Robin did not find it easy to get his blows in, and the stranger found that Robin parried his strokes with ease and deftness. Little John watched in delight, for he well remembered how he himself had fought with Robin over the stream, and short of fighting his master himself, he loved to see someone else trying his strength with him.

To and fro went the fighters, kicking up such a dust that Little John could hardly see them at times. Robin got three blows home, and Little John marvelled that each one of them did not fell the other to the ground, for few could withstand

Robin at his best. The stranger struck his foe twice. The first blow took Robin on the knuckles, so that his fingers were nearly broken. He could hardly hold his staff, and whilst he was hopping about in pain, the stranger smote him again.

Down went Robin into the dust, and swallowed enough to make him cough and splutter. But in a trice he was up, and faced the stranger once more.

Then Little John ran out of the bushes, for he would not

Little John watched in delight.

see his master hurt again. He caught hold of the stranger's staff, and cried to him to stop.

"I am fighting fairly," said the man. "I would not strike him when he was down. Are there any more of you in the hedge? Bring them all out, and I'll fight every one of you!"

"Nay!" cried Robin. "You'll fight no more with me or my friends! You are a good fellow and a fine fighter. Neither I nor my men shall molest you henceforth!"

The stranger stood near by and looked at Robin closely.

Little John looked at his master and began to laugh—and, indeed, Robin was a droll sight. He was covered with dust, one of his long hose had slipped down, his sleeve was torn, and his face streaked with dirt. He ran to the stream and washed himself, while the stranger stood near by and looked at him closely.

"By my troth!" he said at last; "I can put a name to you. You are the famous Robin Hood."

"You speak truth," said Robin, "but I do not feel famous to-day."

"Now how came it that I did not know you?" said the stranger. "If only I had, we need not have fought. Say, lad, do you not know me?"

Robin looked at the scarlet youth closely. Then suddenly he threw his arms around him and embraced him in delight.

"Will! Cousin Will!" he cried. "Now, how could I not have known you?"

It was indeed his cousin, he who had been Robin's best friend in the days gone by. Eagerly Robin questioned him, asking why he had come to seek him.

"I am an outlaw," he said to Will. "You are not safe with me."

"I, too, am an outlaw now," said Will. "I have broken the law, and the Sheriff is after me, and would clap me into prison could he find me. So I thought I would come to seek you, Robin, and join your merry company."

"Then you are right welcome," said Robin gladly. "See, this is Little John, my chief man."

"Shake hands with me, Little John," said Will, "for I have heard of your fame, and would be honoured to have your hand in mine."

"Here's my hand," said Little John heartily. "What is your second name, Will?"

"We will call him Will Scarlet!" cried Robin. "He came to us clad in scarlet, and that shall be his name henceforth. Welcome to our company, Will Scarlet!"

Then all of them clasped hands again, and gladly they swore to be true to each other. Thus did Robin find his second chief man, Will Scarlet.

The Wedding of Allen-a-Dale

Robin Hood was out walking one day, when he met a gay young knight dressed, like Will Scarlet, all in red. He seemed very joyful, and sang a merry song as he walked. His voice was very sweet, and Robin stepped behind a tree to listen, for he loved music.

Robin told his men of the sweet-voiced knight, and bade them seize him if they met him, for he would have speech with him.

The next day Little John and Much, the miller's son, went walking together. Very droll they looked, for Little John was almost a giant and Much was nearly a dwarf. As they went through the forest, they met the same knight that Robin had seen and heard the day before.

But how different he was! No longer was he dressed so gaily, but in a suit of sombre grey. His head was bent and his steps were slow. He sang no song, but sighed dolefully.

Little John and Much stepped out and caught his arms. Then they led him off to Robin Hood, as they had been commanded. The knight was surprised and angered to find himself seized, but he could not free himself from Little John's strong grasp, and soon he was standing before Robin Hood.

" How now ! " said Robin in surprise. " Can it be that you are the same knight I saw yesterday, clad in scarlet, and singing a merry song ? "

" I am the same," answered the knight sadly.

" What has happened to change your merry looks ? " asked Robin. " Tell me your tale, good fellow, for mayhap I can help you."

"I am a poor knight," said the man. "My name is Allen-a-Dale, and I was pledged to a sweet maid. For seven years have I waited to wed her, and yesterday was to have been my wedding-day. But a rich old knight is favoured by her father, and to-day he is to wed my maid. Do you wonder that I am sad?"

"Can you not fight him?" asked Robin.

But how different he was!

"He is shut up in his castle," said Allen. "I went to speak with him yesterday, and he would not let me come near him, but sent his servants to throw me into the moat. I have no men, and can do nothing to save my true love."

"Does she love you?" asked Robin.

"That she does," said the young man. "And she is as sad as I, for why should sweet May wed chill December?"

"What will you give me if I help you to your true love again?" asked Robin. "Have you gold?"

"Alas! I have but five shillings," said Allen-a-Dale. "But, good Robin Hood, if you will but help me, I will be your man from henceforth, and serve you faithfully in the Greenwood. I am not skilful with sword or bow, but I can make sweet music, and sing songs to delight your heart."

Robin was glad to hear that, for he had often wished for a minstrel among his company. He bade Allen be of good cheer, and promised to help him.

"Where is the wedding, and at what time?" he asked.

"At Plympton Church, five miles away, and the time three o'clock this afternoon," answered Allen.

"Then to Plympton Church we go!" cried Robin Hood, leaping up. "Twenty-four men shall be outside the church at three o'clock, and with them you must come, Allen-a-Dale. Men, see that you deck him out as bravely as yourselves. Friar Tuck shall go ahead of all of us, and make his way into the back of the church, there to await my orders."

Robin set Friar Tuck on his way, and then disguised himself as a minstrel. He borrowed Allen-a-Dale's harp, and set off to Plympton. When he arrived there, he found that many of the guests had already assembled, and were sitting in the church. Friar Tuck was also there, seated at the back, looking very saintly indeed.

At the door, newly arrived, was the fat Bishop of Hereford, who was to marry the bride to the old knight. He looked angrily at the minstrel, and spoke to him sharply.

"Now, what do you here?" he said.

"I am but a minstrel," answered Robin. "I heard that there was to be a grand wedding to-day, so I came to see if I might make a song about it."

"Let me hear you play," said the Bishop.

"When the bride and bridegroom are married, but not

before," answered Robin. "To play on my harp now might bring ill fortune to both."

At that moment the bridal party arrived. First came the old knight, decked out in white satin, that sat ill on his bent figure. His countenance was sharp and wrinkled, and old age frowned there.

Then came the sweet bride, young and fair. Her eyes shone like dewy violets, and her hair was a sheet of gold. She had

Friar Tuck was also there, looking very saintly.

been weeping, and still looked sad, so that all the women in the church sorrowed for her, and wished that she could have married her own true love.

The bride and bridegroom stood before the altar rails, and the Bishop opened his book to begin the marriage service. But at that moment Robin Hood strode up the aisle, and stood beside the bride.

"Hold!" he said. "I forbid this wedding!"

"What do you mean, fellow?" demanded the Bishop angrily, and he beckoned to his liveried servants to throw Robin out. "Were you not the minstrel?"

"Yes," answered Robin. "And now I will play you some music."

He put his horn to his lips and blew three loud blasts. Then every one knew that he was the famous Robin Hood, and eagerly they pushed forward, trying to see him. The servants rushed to seize Robin, but, drawing his bow, he kept them at bay.

"Come no farther!" he cried. "And you, wedding guests, keep your seats, for you shall see the bride married. But she shall choose her own groom."

Then all Robin's men came running into the church, and soon had the servants pinned down so that they could do nothing. First of the men was Allen-a-Dale, and he ran straight to where his maiden stood, frightened and amazed, by the altar rails.

"Sweet maiden," said Robin Hood, "look round the church, and choose who you will have for your husband."

The maid glanced at Allen-a-Dale and then clasped her arms about his neck in joy.

"The lady has made her choice," said Robin gaily. "Lord Bishop, you may go on with the wedding."

"That will I not!" said the Bishop angrily. "You know as well as I that the banns must be called three times in church before a couple may be wedded. I will not marry them."

"Very well; we will find someone else," said Robin, with a laugh. "Ho, Friar Tuck, come forward. You shall call the banns for the marriage, and marry the couple too."

Then Friar Tuck came forward, big and burly. Robin pulled off the Bishop's fine gown, and put it on the Friar, who looked very comical in it, because he was far bigger than the Bishop. Then Friar Tuck called the banns seven times, in case three were not enough, and everyone began to laugh, to hear his jolly voice ringing through the church.

"Do not laugh, people," said Friar Tuck, pretending to be shocked. "That is not the right thing to do in church. Now, who gives this maiden in marriage?"

"I do!" said Robin Hood; "I, Robin Hood of Sherwood."

Clasped her arms about his neck in joy.

Then the maiden and Allen-a-Dale knelt down before Friar Tuck, and he married them there and then. After the wedding all the Merry Men took Allen and his wife to the forest, and there they found a splendid feast awaiting them.

Never was there such a merry wedding, and long was it talked of. Allen kept his word to Robin, and he and his pretty young wife went to live in the Greenwood, and served Robin faithfully. Very happy were they both, and often Allen-a-Dale played and sang to the Merry Men, making the woods echo to the sound of his tuneful voice.

Robin Hood and the Bishop

ONE MORNING Arthur-a-Bland came running to Robin Hood, and told him that the Bishop of Hereford was going to pass that way in the afternoon.

"Ho!" said Robin, twanging his bow, "then we will play a trick on him. Fetch shepherd-clothes, my Merry Men, and we will disguise ourselves so that he will not know us."

Very soon Robin and six of his men were dressed in smocks and wide-brimmed hats. They rubbed dirt on their faces, and a funnier lot of shepherds never were seen.

"Kill a deer and carry it to the highway down which the Bishop will pass," said Robin. "We will cook it there, and see his anger when he comes riding by!"

So Will Scarlet shot a deer, and dragged it to the side of the road. Much, the miller's son, lighted a fire, and soon the deer was being cooked. Robin kept a good look-out for the Bishop, and at last saw a cloud of dust in the distance.

"Here he comes!" he cried. "And ten armed men with him. We shall have some sport."

Out of the dust came the Bishop of Hereford, cantering gaily through the forest feeling quite safe with his company of armed men behind him. When he saw the shepherds by the wayside he drew in his horse and stopped.

"What!" he cried; "do you dare to eat the King's deer? Who are you, fellows?"

"Shepherds, your Honour," answered Robin, grinning in a sheepish manner.

"A sorry lot you look!" said the Bishop, with a sneer. "Who gave you leave to feast on deer? Answer me that, knave!"

"None gave us leave," answered Robin boldly. "We were tired of mutton, and thought a taste of venison would be welcome. Does it not smell good, your Honour?"

The Bishop went purple in the face.

"How *dare* you kill the King's deer?" he shouted. "You shall suffer for this, you saucy fellows! I command you to march with my men, and I will see that you pay for this with your lives!"

Robin kept a good look-out.

"Pardon, pardon; I crave pardon!" cried Robin, dropping upon his knees, and pretending to be terrified. "Do not rob seven men of their lives."

"No pardon shall you have from me!" answered the fat Bishop fiercely. "Get up, and go with my men!"

The Bishop's servants sprang to seize Robin and the others, but in a trice the outlaw leapt away. From beneath his shepherd's dress he drew his horn, and three times he blew upon it to summon his trusty men to his side.

At once they appeared from the bushes round about, where he had bade them hide. The astonished Bishop saw scores of men in Lincoln green running to Robin. They dropped upon their knees, and asked his bidding.

Robin threw off his shepherd's dress, and showed himself in his Lincoln green. He ordered his men to seize the arms of the Bishop's servants, and to take the Bishop himself a prisoner.

" Pardon ! I crave pardon !" cried Robin.

"Oh, pardon !" said the terrified man. "Oh, pardon, I pray you. Set me free, and I will never come this way again."

"No pardon shall you have from me !" cried Robin, using the same words to the Bishop as the Bishop had used to him. "Would you have spared the lives of seven men ? Nay, you would have put each man to death. Why should I not slay you in return ?"

Then the Bishop's fat cheeks went as white as a sheet, and he shook in his saddle.

" But be not afraid," said Robin, pleased to see that he had given the priest a moment's real terror; " I will not treat you as badly as you would have treated me. Come; you shall dine with me this day. Will, put the half-cooked meat at the back of the Bishop and his horse shall carry both."

The meat was flung behind the Bishop, and then Robin led the way to the open space where he and his men loved to feast and make merry.

" Take a seat upon the grass," said Robin courteously. " The meal will soon be ready."

The Bishop sat down, and, angry and fearful though he was, he could not help sniffing gladly at the delicious smell that arose from the roasting meat. Robin placed a full plate before him, and asked him to say grace for them.

The Bishop obeyed. Then all the men fell to with good appetite, and the Bishop ate as heartily as any. Many were the jests that were tossed about, and loud was the laughter. Even the Bishop could not help smiling sometimes.

When the meal was finished, he began to feel uncomfortable. Would Robin Hood make him pay very highly for his dinner? He remembered that the Sheriff had had to pay twenty gold pieces, and he hoped Robin would charge him no more than that. He had no less than four hundred gold pieces in his saddle-bags, which he had taken from a poor knight in order to enrich himself. He trembled at the thought of them, and wished heartily that he had come a different way through the forest that day.

" Robin Hood," said the Bishop, standing up, " you have given me a good dinner. Now I will pay the bill and go. It is getting late, and I fear that the cost of this entertainment will be too heavy for me to pay if I stay any longer."

" Really, your Honour," said Robin, smiling broadly, " I have so much enjoyed having you here under the Greenwood Tree that I do not know how much to charge you ! "

"Give me your purse," said Little John; "I will then see how much you can afford."

"I have only a few shillings of my own," said the trembling Bishop. "As for the gold in my saddle-bags, that is not mine. It belongs to the Church. You cannot touch that, my friends."

But Little John only laughed. He went straight to the saddle-bags and took them. Then he spread the Bishop's cloak upon the ground and emptied the bags upon it. Out rolled four hundred glittering pieces of gold!

"Ha!" said Robin, much pleased. "This money has put a plan into my mind. I have no doubt that you have taken it from people who can ill afford to give it, your Lordship; so I, in my turn, will take it, and promise you I will give it to the poor folk whose hearts are heavy and whose purses are light. Take it, Little John."

"Nay," said the Bishop, almost weeping. "Leave me some. I am a poor man."

"You lie," said Robin sternly. "You are very rich, for all the countryside tells of your oppression. "You, as a bishop, should use your money to help the poor and needy; but instead you take from them what little they have. For shame, my lord!"

The Bishop glowered at Little John as he counted out the money, and gave it to one of the Merry Men to stow safely away. Robin looked upon his surly face and laughed.

"Ho!" he cried. "The Bishop looks sad! Let us gladden him a little. Now, Bishop, which will you do—sing or dance?"

"Neither!" snapped the Bishop in a fury.

"Well, you shall dance then!" said Little John, winking at Robin. He seized the fat old man, and began to jig him round and round and up and down, whilst Allen-a-Dale played a merry tune on his harp. Then all the men rolled on the ground, and laughed till the tears ran down their cheeks to see the Bishop's antics.

Began to jig him round and round.

At last he fell to the ground, giddy and tired out. Little John picked him up, carried him to his horse, and sat him on it, with his face to the tail. Then he led the horse to the highway, and sent it trotting off to Nottingham.

"He will not come here again!" said Robin, laughing. "Of a surety that was the dearest meal he ever bought!"

How the Bishop hunted Robin Hood

ROBIN HOOD was so certain that the Bishop of Hereford would not dare to come back into the forest to punish him for taking away his bags of gold, that he went out alone, far from his Merry Men. The day was a lovely one, and the birds were singing beautifully. Robin wandered along, his bow and arrow in his hands, listening to the blackbird and the thrush.

But the Bishop was so angry because his gold had been stolen, that he determined to take a company of armed men with him, and hunt Robin till he caught him. That very morning he had been to see the Sheriff of Nottingham, and had offered to double the price set on the outlaw's head if the Sheriff would give him a large company of his soldiers to take into Sherwood Forest.

The Sheriff agreed. There was nothing he wanted more than to see Robin caught and hanged. So off set the Bishop, with a troop of soldiers at his heels, eager to find the famous outlaw and catch him.

Robin had no idea of this. He thought himself quite safe. He wandered along alone, and at last stood under an oak tree listening to a bird in the branches above.

At that moment the Bishop and his men came galloping along the road. Robin Hood, taken by surprise, peered to see who it was with such a large company. He and the Bishop saw each other at the same moment, and both were full of astonishment. In a trice the Bishop saw that Robin was alone, and that he had a splendid chance of taking the outlaw with the greatest ease.

Robin Hood peered to see.

"There's Robin Hood!" he shouted to his men. "See; there he stands yonder! Ride at him, men, and you will take him easily, for he is alone! Ride, ride!"

What was Robin to do? His men were too far away to hear his horn, and he could not fight a large company of armed men by himself. He would be caught and hanged.

"That will I not!" cried Robin in a fury. He dodged behind the tree, and then took to his heels and ran with all his might. Behind came the soldiers, crashing through the bushes, making their way through the trees with difficulty; but still they gained upon Robin Hood, and he, glancing behind, saw that they would soon be on him.

He ran to where the trees grew thicker and the undergrowth was matted and tangled. The horses found it very difficult to follow, and fell to a walk, whilst their riders tried to find the easiest way between the crowded trees. The Bishop had been left behind with a few men, and he followed slowly, not wishing to be at the front in case the Merry Men should suddenly come to rescue their leader.

Robin was very hard pressed. He was running away from the part of the wood where his men were, and he knew that when he came into the clearer part again, the horses would gain upon him. Then he suddenly remembered an old woman's cottage not very far away. He would go there.

On he ran, and left the soldiers behind. He soon came to the cottage, and rapped on the door.

"Who is there?" asked a quavering voice.

"It is I, Robin Hood!" panted the outlaw. "The Sheriff's soldiers are at my heels, good dame."

"Come in, come in!" cried the old woman, opening the door at once. "Let me see your face. Ah, you are indeed the good Robin Hood! Now welcome, welcome! This old woman will do all she can for you, for did not your men bring me fine shoes and stockings only last week? And when I was ill and a-bed, did they not bring me bread and meat, and chop my firewood for me ? Therefore thrice welcome, good Robin! "

Robin stepped indoors, and the old woman bolted the door.

" Listen, dame," said Robin. " Will you give me an old dress of yours and a cloak and cap ? Then I will put them on, and go from this cottage in safety."

" That will I! " cried the old dame. " And I will myself wear your Lincoln green, Robin ; then when the men come they will think I am you—thus you will have a good start, and will escape."

" Good mother, I will never forget your help," cried Robin, stripping off his suit, and swiftly putting on the old woman's things. " You need have no fear, for I and my men will shortly return here to rescue you, if you are taken. Bolt your door, and wait for us."

The brave old woman laughed to see Robin in her clothes. Then, hearing the noise of horses near by, she quickly let him out of the back door, thrusting into his hand her spindle and a good stout stick. Then she bolted the door and set to work to dress herself in Robin's Lincoln green. She pulled his hat well down over her face, and flung his mantle around her thin shoulders. Then she waited to see what would happen, her heart beating faster than it had done since her young days.

Meanwhile Robin was hobbling through the trees, his back bent and his steps slow, like an old woman's. He muttered and mumbled to himself as he went, for all the world like a poor old dame. Soon the Bishop's men caught sight of him. Robin heard them around him, but he did not dare to hasten his steps, or he would have given himself away. On he went, mumbling all the time.

At first the men took no notice of the grey-clad figure, but continued their search for Robin. The Bishop, who rode up at that moment, saw the old woman, and called to his men to catch her and question her.

"Ask her if she has seen Robin Hood," he commanded.

So a soldier rode up to the old woman and caught hold of her arm.

"Let me be! let me be!" croaked Robin Hood in a hoarse voice. "If you will not leave go my arm, I will curse you with a dreadful curse!"

The soldier was afraid, for he thought the old woman might

He did not dare to hasten.

be a witch. He let go his hold on her arm, and spoke gently to her.

"Do not be afraid, old dame," he said. "The Bishop wants to know if you have seen Robin Hood. I'll not hurt you, so do not curse me."

"What harm is it if I do see Robin Hood?" said the seeming old woman in a whining voice. "He brings me food and clothing, and when has the Bishop of Hereford ever done that for any of the poor folk in the forest?"

"Silence, woman!" commanded the Bishop angrily. "Do you want to be burnt as a witch? Tell me at once, when last you saw Robin Hood."

"Oh, mercy, mercy!" said the old dame, falling on her knees. "Your Lordship, Robin Hood is in my cottage now, but spare him, I pray you, for he has done no harm, but only good to me."

"Ha!" cried the Bishop, wheeling his horse about in joy. "In the cottage, you say! Now we have him, my men! Let the old dame go on her way. Surround the cottage, and batter down the door. I'll give a purse of gold to the man who captures the outlaw alive!"

The soldiers released the pretended old woman and rode eagerly to the cottage. Robin Hood arose from his knees, thankful to escape so easily, and went hobbling on his way. He waited until he had left the Bishop's men well behind, and then he fairly ran to where he knew his men would be awaiting him.

He had to go a long way, but at last he saw Little John and the others in the distance. They saw him too, but did not know him to be their master, for they thought he was an old woman. They were amazed to see an old dame striding along so swiftly, and thought surely she must be a witch. Little John fitted an arrow to his bow and aimed it just above the woman's head.

"If she's a witch, she'll mount on her stick and fly away!" he cried.

Robin heard the arrow whistle by his head, and cried out loudly to Little John.

"Hold your hand! hold your hand!" he panted, throwing off the old dame's cap he wore, and showing his curly head beneath. "It is I, Robin Hood! Shoot no more!"

"Master, master, I might have shot you!" cried Little John. "What do you, dressed like this?"

"I will tell you soon," said Robin, trying to get his breath. "Summon the men, Little John, and tell them to follow speedily on my heels. The Bishop of Hereford is in the forest with the Sheriff's soldiers."

Little John summoned all the Merry Men, and they came running to Robin, grinning to see their master in such queer dress. He quickly stripped off his skirts and donned another suit. Then swiftly the outlaw raced back to the old woman's cottage, to rescue her.

Meanwhile she had been having a most exciting time. The soldiers had tried to batter down her door, but it was strong, and for some time they could not break it.

"Batter it! batter it!" cried the Bishop in a fury. "Fetch out that traitor! There is gold waiting for the first man in!"

With a crash the door fell in, and the way was clear. But at first no man dared to cross the threshold, for each was afraid of being pierced by an arrow. Then, as all seemed silent in the cottage, one man peered in. He saw a green-coated figure standing at the far end, and he cried out in triumph:

"We have him! we have him! He is there in the corner!"

Then the men all rushed in, and caught hold of the figure in the green mantle, thinking it was Robin Hood; but of course it was really the old woman! She was enjoying herself, and with her stick she laid about her with a right good will, giving many a man a good crack over the pate. At last they held both her arms, and dragged her out of the cottage to the Bishop. She held her head well down, for she did not want him to see that she was not Robin Hood.

"See how he hangs his head in shame!" cried the Bishop, rubbing his hands in joy. "So, Robin Hood, I have you at last! Say farewell to the Greenwood, for never again will you see it!"

The old woman said not a word. She knew that if she spoke

her secret would be out, and she did not want anyone to guess it until Robin Hood came to rescue her, as he had promised.

"This is the prince of robbers," said the Bishop, pointing at the old woman. "We will set him on a princely horse, and let him ride by my side into Nottingham."

So the finest horse in the company was brought, and the old woman was heaved up on to its milk-white back and tied

She laid about her with a right good will.

firmly there, in case of escape. The soldiers who tied her on looked up into her downcast face, and marvelled to see it.

"Robin Hood is ugly!" said one.

"It is the wicked life he leads!" said the other. This made the old dame shake with anger, but still she said never a word.

Then the Bishop sounded the call for all the rest of his men to join him, and off they set. The old dame jogged along on the milk-white horse beside the Bishop's dappled pony, wondering when Robin would come to save her.

Now as they all rode along, light of heart to think that they had caught Robin Hood, and would be rewarded by gold, the soldiers caught sight of a hundred men in Lincoln green standing silently beneath a large oak tree by the wayside. The Bishop saw them too, and he turned pale. Still, he had Robin Hood safe, and if these men tried to rescue him, he would have the outlaw slain outright.

" Who are these ? " he said aloud. " And who is it that leads them ? "

" By my faith," said the old woman, speaking for the first time, " I think it is a man called Robin Hood ! "

" Then who are you, that I have here with me ? " demanded the Bishop, turning to the woman in dismay.

" Only an old woman, my lord," said the dame, looking at the Bishop—and he saw that she spoke the truth. It was not Robin Hood that he had by his side.

Then the Bishop's heart misgave him sorely.

" Woe is me that ever I saw this day ! " he cried, and wheeled his horse about, to flee away.

But Robin had run up to him, and now laid a firm hand on his bridle.

" Not so fast, my lord," he said, doffing his cap politely. " Where is the purse of gold that you were going to give to the first man who took me alive ? Give it to this brave old dame, and it will pay for a new door to her cottage. Oh, fie, my lord ! To think that you should batter down a poor woman's door ! Such a deed ill becomes the Bishop of Hereford ! "

The Bishop looked round at his soldiers. He saw that they had all laid down their weapons, and that Robin's men were guarding them. There was no hope for him, and no escape. He must give the old dame his purse. He took it from his girdle, and flung it down to the ground. Then, with a cry of rage, he turned his horse about and fled down the road.

Robin let him go, and all that followed the furious Bishop was a burst of mocking laughter from the Merry Men.

"Let me untie your bonds, mother," said Robin Hood. "You are as brave as any of my company. A thousand thanks to you, and be sure that neither I nor my men will ever forget this day. See, here is the Bishop's purse. His gold will keep you in comfort for many a week. Now come with us, and we

Off rode the old dame.

will feast you beneath the Greenwood Tree, for such a deed as yours deserves all we can give."

Then off rode the old dame in her Lincoln green cloak and feathered hat, while all the Merry Men followed joyfully. They took with them the weapons belonging to the Sheriff's soldiers, who went back to Nottingham full of wrath to think that they had had Robin Hood under their hands, and had unwittingly let him go.

As for the Bishop of Hereford, no one ventured near him for two days, so angry was he, and never again did he go hunting for outlaws in the Forest of Sherwood!

Robin Hood and Maid Marian

ROBIN HOOD often thought of sweet Maid Marian, with whom he used to play in the Greenwood, when he and Will Scarlet were boys. He had loved her then, and he loved her still. But she was a maid of high degree, and how could an outlaw ask such a maid to come and live in the forest? She was used to palaces and fine folk; she could not live the rough life of the Merry Men.

As often as Robin Hood thought of Maid Marian, so often and more did she think of him. She had had a letter from him, which he had sent when his home had been burnt and his father slain, bidding her good-bye, telling her that now he was an outlaw—and this letter Marian kept, and read often, when she thought of Robin.

At last she could no longer live her life without at least seeing him once more. She was unhappy, and could find no pleasure in anything. So she resolved to disguise herself, and go to seek her love in Sherwood Forest.

She dressed herself as a page, and put on sword and buckler. She carried with her a bow and arrows, and thus armed she set off to Sherwood. She knew that a maid could not wander alone in the forest, but thought that a page-boy would go unmolested.

Now it so happened that Robin Hood was that day in the forest, also disguised. He had been to Nottingham, and was now returning, whistling merrily, his sword swinging by his side. Soon he and the page met in the same narrow path, and Robin called upon the youth to halt.

Marian, forgetting that she was supposed to be a page, was angered that a man should show her so little courtesy as not to allow her to pass. She would not halt, but tried to press by Robin, who was so well disguised that she did not know him.

"Halt, I said!" cried the outlaw angrily, and he seized Marian's arm. In a trice she whipped out her sword.

"Ho!" said Robin. "You wish to fight? Come then, bold youth!"

The two fought together.

Then he drew his sword also, and the two began to fight. Robin was gentle with the page, for he saw that he was young and slender, and he admired his bravery. But the youngster was angry at Robin's gentleness, and attacked him all the more fiercely. She was very clever with the sword, and Robin could not admire enough the way the young page fought.

"If only he were one of my men," he thought, "I should be proud of him indeed! He is so quick and so deft."

For nearly an hour the two fought together. By that time Robin had a slight wound in the cheek, and Marian was wounded in the arm. The maid was getting tired, and Robin saw that the page's strokes were weakening.

"Now hold your hand," he said gently. "You shall be one of my men, if you will. You shall roam in the forest and hear the birds sing with me and my Merry Men."

"Then—you must be Robin Hood!" cried Maid Marian, catching her breath in wonder, marvelling that she had not seen through his disguise before.

Robin looked at the page closely, and his heart gave a leap at the sound of her voice, which he knew at once.

"Marian!" he cried in joy. "Maid Marian! Is it really you? Oh, my love, I have hurt you! Let me bathe your arm. How did you come here—tell me all!"

He took the page to the stream, and tenderly he bathed her bleeding arm, and she as lovingly bathed his cheek.

Each told the other all that had happened since they had last met, and they laughed and kissed in joy.

"I came to seek you in the Greenwood," said Marian. "And when I found you I did not know you!"

"Nor I you!" said Robin. "Oh, Marian, how shall I live when you leave the Greenwood, and return again to your home?"

"I will never go back," said Maid Marian, "I will stay here with you. Does not the Lady Christabel, wife to Allen-a-Dale, live with you and the Merry Men? Then why should not I?"

"Ah, Marian, you are not used to the rough life we lead," said Robin.

"That matters nothing," said Marian. "I shall be with you, and we will be happy together."

So Robin joyfully agreed to have Maid Marian in his company, and resolved to get Friar Tuck to marry them that self-same day. Together they wandered through the forest to the open space where his men awaited their leader. How they stared when they saw their master hand-in-hand with a slender page!

Little John went to meet them, and so big he seemed that Maid Marian clutched Robin's hand in fear.

"Do not be afraid," said he, laughing. "This is my first man, faithful Little John. He will guard you well when I go hunting through the forest, and will be as loyal to you as to me. Now, Little John, down on your knees to Maid Marian, my own true love!"

Little John gaped in surprise to see a maid dressed in page's clothes, but down he dropped to do her homage. Then all the Merry Men came too, and swore to serve the maid faithfully and well, and to be as loyal to her as they were to Robin. She should be their lovely Queen, they vowed.

"We must have a feast to-day such as we have never had before," cried Little John. "I will take my bow and arrows, Master, and see what I can find for our cooks!"

So off he went through the forest to kill some fat deer to grace the wedding-feast of Robin Hood and Maid Marian. Allen-a-Dale's wife took the maid with her to give her a dress of Lincoln green, and soon there was no longer a page-boy, but sweet Marian herself, blushing in a fine dress of green velvet, as pretty a sight as had ever been seen in the Greenwood before.

Then Friar Tuck was called, and there in the forest, before all the Merry Men, Robin Hood and Maid Marian were wed. After the wedding came the marriage-feast, laid on snowy-white cloths spread on the grass. Never had there been such a feast! The cooks had done their work well, and the cloths were laden with delicious meats. At the end Robin leapt to his feet.

"Drink a health to Maid Marian, Queen of the Greenwood!"
he shouted, and emptied his drinking-horn at a draught. All
the Merry Men sprang to their feet also, and drank their lovely
Queen's health. There they all stood, tall and strong, gay in
their suits of Lincoln green. They waved their hats and

As pretty a sight as had ever been seen in the Greenwood.

cheered till the forest echoed, and all the birds were silent
with amaze.

Then Allen-a-Dale struck the strings of his harp, and every
one began to dance. Robin and Marian danced too, happier
than ever they had been in their lives before.

Thus did Maid Marian come to live in the Greenwood,
and long and happily did she and Robin dwell together.

The Golden Arrow

No MATTER what the Sheriff did, he could not catch Robin Hood. He hated to think that the outlaw was merrily treading the Greenwood, laughing because the Sheriff could not catch him. So at last he made up his mind to go to London and complain to the King.

" Then perhaps he will let me have more soldiers," thought the Sheriff.

So he set off, taking with him a large company of servants and soldiers, for he feared to be set upon and robbed on the way. He arrived safely in London, and sent a messenger to the King.

" I will see this Sheriff," said the King, and he sent for him to come the next day.

The Sheriff, dressed in his grandest clothes, bowed his way into the King's presence.

" What have you to say to me ? " asked the King.

" Sire, I come to complain of an outlaw, Robin Hood, who dwells in Sherwood Forest with many scores of men, all of whom own him master and obey him. They feast on Your Majesty's deer, and laugh at my commands to cease their evil ways. They rob the rich, and give the money to the poor. Often have I tried——"

" Have you no soldiers at Nottingham ? " asked the King.

" Yes," answered the Sheriff.

" Then why cannot you catch this outlaw ? " asked the King sharply. " Why do you come to me ? "

" To ask for more soldiers, Your Majesty," stammered the Sheriff.

" I can give you no more," said the King. " You waste my time, Sheriff. If you cannot with your soldiers catch this outlaw, either by force or by trickery, then you are no good sheriff. Go back to Nottingham, and plague me no more. If you cannot capture Robin Hood, I will put another man in your place, be sure of that."

The Sheriff bowed his way out, red in the face and full of dismay. He had thought that the King would give him scores of soldiers and feast him royally—but instead he had been

" What have you to say to me ? " asked the king.

harshly rebuked, and maybe he would lose his post as Sheriff. How he wished he had not travelled all the way to London !

Back he went to Nottingham, sad and angry. What *could* he do to catch Robin Hood ? He must take him by force or by trickery, the King had said. Well, the Bishop had tried force, and it had failed. Now he, the Sheriff, would try trickery.

He rode back to his house, and shut himself up to think. After a while an idea came into his head.

"I will proclaim a great shooting-match, to see who is

the best archer in the county!" he said. "Robin Hood and his men will be sure to come to it, for they are the best bowmen for miles around. I will have all my soldiers guarding the gates, and then as soon as I see the men in Lincoln green, I will give the signal, and they shall be surrounded! Now this is a good plan; of that I am sure."

He rubbed his hands in glee, and called for the captain of his soldiers. He told him his plan, and the captain agreed that it was good.

"Robin Hood will come!" said he. "Naught will deter him, for he is the best archer in the district. He is no coward, and even though he may guess we shall look for him, he will come. This is a good plan, Sheriff."

"I will offer a beautiful prize to the best archer," said the Sheriff. "It shall be a silver-shafted arrow with a golden head, fine enough to tempt Robin Hood from his lair."

He sent for an old arrow-maker, and told him what he wanted.

"It must be of fine workmanship," he said. "See that you bring it in time for the match."

The arrow-maker promised and went to his home to make the beautiful arrow. Then the Sheriff sent out a proclamation to say that he would hold, in the city of Nottingham, a shooting-match to find the best archer. Anyone could enter for the match, and the prize would be a golden arrow.

The news soon came to Robin Hood and his men.

"Ha!" said bold Robin. "We will go, my men, and show the Sheriff our shooting. We will win his arrow, and fill him with dismay and anger."

The Merry Men cried out with joy, and threw their hats into the air. But at that moment there ran up David of Doncaster, who had just returned from Nottingham.

"Master," he said to Robin, "have you heard of the Sheriff's shooting-match?"

" That have I," cried Robin, " and we are all going ! "

" Nay, that must not be," said David. " It is all a plot of the Sheriff's to get us into Nottingham. He will have his soldiers watching, and we shall be taken. I have heard this to-day, and I come to warn you."

" You talk like a coward ! " said Robin Hood. " We shall go, no matter what plot the Sheriff has made ! "

" Nay, Master ; that were folly to walk into the Sheriff's trap," said Little John. " David's warning is well meant, and he is no coward."

" You talk like a coward ! " said Robin.

" You say true," said Robin. " Come, David lad, tell us what you know."

So David told all he had heard, and soon every man was agreed that they could not go to Nottingham to shoot on that day, for their Lincoln green would give them away.

" Yet how I should like to go ! " sighed Robin.

" I have it, Master ! " cried Little John. " Let us all dress ourselves in suits of different colours, then none will know us, and we shall be able to shoot in safety. One shall wear white, another red, one yellow, another blue."

"We will do it!" said Robin, clapping Little John on his broad shoulder. "What fine sport we shall have!"

Then every day until the match the Merry Men practised their shooting. The twang of the bows and the whir of the arrows were heard on all sides. David was sent into Notting-

Soon gay suits were ready.

ham to buy cloth of many colours, and soon gay suits were ready for the men to wear.

"I shall wear red!" said Robin.

"And I yellow!" cried David.

"Blue for me!" said Little John.

"To-morrow is the day!" cried Robin. "Be up with the lark, my men, and I will give you my commands for the day!"

The Shooting-match

A T LAST the great day dawned, fair and fine. All the men were up early, whistling and singing gaily. Each donned his new suit and laid aside his Lincoln green. Then, taking their bows, they lined up before Robin.

He was in brave scarlet, and looked very fine. He stood in front of his men, and spoke gaily to them.

" Now we go to Nottingham ! " he said. " There will be many strangers going in from the villages all about. We will mix with them, and the Sheriff will not know us. He will be looking for our Lincoln green, and for a band of men all together. Therefore we will go separately, or in twos and threes, and we will behave like country folk, laughing boisterously and playing clownishly. See that you have your bows ready lest the Sheriff recognise us, and some of you must stay about the gates so that they may not be shut upon us."

" We will obey you, Master ! " shouted the men. Then they broke up their lines, and made off in the direction of Nottingham. They hid behind the trees that lined the highway until they saw little groups of country folk, dressed in their best, going that way ; then they mixed with them, in twos and threes, laughing and talking to the men and women as if they were villagers themselves.

The Sheriff was excited and anxious. He was quite certain that Robin and his men would come. He had a large force of soldiers posted at the gates, ready to shut them as soon as the outlaws should be inside. He himself, placed on a high chair, with his pretty wife beside him, watched the crowd pouring into the city, and looked in vain for the Lincoln green of the outlaws.

"There be many hundreds come to see our shooting-match," murmured his wife, as she saw the crowds. " Had we not better begin the shooting soon, my love, or we shall never finish ? "

" Hold your peace ! " growled the Sheriff harshly. " I will not begin until Robin and his men are here."

Again and again he scanned the crowds below him, and at last he beckoned to the captain of the soldiers.

" Is there any sign of the outlaws ? " he asked.

" None, your Honour," answered the Captain gloomily. " Not one man in Lincoln green has passed the gates."

" Has any large group of men come in together ? " questioned the Sheriff.

" No," said the Captain. " The people have come in twos and threes, or else in batches from the outlying villages. Robin's men are not here."

"I would not have thought that the outlaw was coward enough not to come," said the Sheriff. "Well, we must begin the match, for the people get impatient. Are there many archers ? "

" A great number," said the Captain. " I will send word for them to assemble near the targets, and then we will begin."

" My golden arrow will be wasted ! " groaned the Sheriff to himself. " It was only a bait for Robin Hood, and now it will be won by a peasant. I meant to catch the outlaw as soon as he entered the gates, then to declare the match off, and keep the arrow myself. Alas, the money I spent on it is thrown away ! "

The archers were soon assembled near the targets, and every one had a good look at them. There were many men from the nearby villages, with their good yew bows, and some from Nottingham itself. There were also all Robin's men, save those left by the gates. None of them spoke to one another, and little did the Sheriff guess that the men he so much wanted to capture were standing near to him, talking merrily to the village folk.

" Let the match begin ! " cried the Sheriff. " He who strikes the centre of the target oftenest shall have the golden arrow."

So the shooting began. One man after another shot. Robin's men all shot well, and got nearer to the centre of the targets than any one else. If a man missed the target altogether he had to retire, and not shoot any more. The people cheered loudly when any one hit the centre, and soon it was seen that there were some very fine archers shooting that day.

The Sheriff watched the men shooting at the targets, and was astonished to see so many arrows hitting the centre. He had never seen such good shooting before. Soon, as men fell out one by one, there were only Robin and his men left, shooting against one another, as they often did in the Greenwood. They said no word to each other, for fear they might be known—but each man thrilled to think that the people of Nottingham—ay, and the Sheriff too—should be cheering them, the outlaws of Sherwood Forest.

" If Robin Hood were here he could not shoot better than these men ! " cried the watching folk in delight, as Robin sent another arrow right into the centre of his target.

The Sheriff heard the people saying this, and he scratched his head and frowned.

" I thought he would have been here," he said. " I thought he would, but though he's bold, he dare not appear. He is not brave enough for that ! "

Now it so happened that Robin was standing just by the Sheriff, whose seat of honour was behind the archers, so that he might have a good view of the shooting. He heard the Sheriff muttering that he, Robin, was not brave enough to come to the match, and he did not know whether to laugh or to be angry. How he longed to turn round and proclaim himself !

" I'll win the golden arrow," resolved Robin. " I'll take it away with me to the Greenwood, and then somehow I will tell the Sheriff that it is I, Robin Hood, who has taken it—and he will know I am no coward ! "

Still the shooting went on, and the watching people grew even more excited, for never in their lives before had they seen such marvellous shooting.

" Ho, Bluejacket ! " cried one ; " you will win ! "

" Nay, I back Browncoat ! " cried another. " See how straight his arrows fly ! "

Robin sent another right into the centre.

" Brave Yellow ! " cried a third. " Shoot your best ! You will get the prize ! "

" Yon man in red has no fellow ! " shouted a fourth. " Never once have his arrows flown from the centre of the target ! He is the finest archer in the world ! "

Robin Hood was the man in red. By him stood David of Doncaster, clad in yellow. He was very much excited, for he had never shot better in his life, and he had a fair chance of winning the arrow himself.

At last the match was between him and Robin only. With trembling hand young David twanged his bow to send his last arrow. It flew straight and true, almost to the centre of his target. The people cheered him loudly.

Then Robin's strong hand pulled his bow-string. Out sped the arrow, and struck the target fairly in the middle. Robin had won!

It flew straight and true almost to the centre.

The people, excited by such wonderful shooting, ran out on to the field to clap Robin on his back. But they found they could not get near him, for somehow or other many of the other archers grouped themselves round him. They were Robin's men, who, seeing that their master had won the prize, and might be recognised by the Sheriff when he went to receive it, had clustered round him to protect him if the soldiers were sent to take him.

But the Sheriff did not know the outlaw. He looked for men

in green, and seeing none, he had quite made up his mind that Robin was not there.

He bade his wife present the golden arrow to the winner, and she did so. Robin bowed politely and thanked her. Then, with the people cheering him madly, he strolled off into the town to enjoy himself at the Fair held there that day.

Later on, by ones and twos, the outlaws slipped out of the city gates, mixing as before with the villagers. Soon none were left in the city. Robin too was gone, and he hastened to the Greenwood to hear what his men had to say about the day's sport.

How they laughed and joked! How they clapped one another on the back, and told of the day's adventures! The beautiful golden arrow was passed all around the company, and David of Doncaster sighed when he thought how nearly it had been his.

"You shot well, David lad," said Robin, taking the arrow from him—and those few words made up to David for the prize he had missed.

"Did you hear the Sheriff say that we were not brave enough to go to his match?" said Robin to his men.

"Ay," said Little John. "And I nearly gave him a buffet on his pate."

The men laughed loudly. But Robin frowned, for he could not bear to think that the Sheriff might deem him a coward.

"All I care about is that the Sheriff may know that it was I, Robin Hood, who bore his arrow away!" said he.

"Well, I will tell you what you may do," said Little John.

"Speak on," bade Robin.

"Write a letter to the Sheriff," said Little John. "In it you shall say that you were the man in red who took his golden arrow. Tell him that all your Merry Men were there, and that we laughed to see so many soldiers watching for us, when we stood near them all the time!"

"That is good," said Robin, pleased. "But, Little John, how may I get this letter delivered? If I send any of my men, they will be captured before they can get out of the city."

"Write your letter, and I will get it delivered, never fear!" said Little John.

So Robin wrote his letter. Little John took it, and stuck it on an arrow. Then early the next morning, before any one was about, he shot it up into the air in the direction of Nottingham.

He could hardly believe his eyes.

It fell in the street outside the Sheriff's house, and was found by one of his soldiers.

Soon the Sheriff was awakened, and the letter was given to him. When he read it he could hardly believe his eyes. He raved and shouted as if he were mad.

"I laid my trap, and Robin Hood walked into it!" he wailed. "And I let him go free! Oh, was there ever a more unfortunate man than I!"

Robin Hood and the Tinker
of Banbury

To the Sheriff's house one day there came a strolling tinker called Middle. He was sent to the kitchen to mend some pots and pans, and as he worked away he began to boast.

" So the Sheriff had Robin Hood under his hand and let him go ! " he laughed. " Ho ! If *I* had him, he would not escape so easily ! If only I had a warrant for his arrest, I would find him and bring him to the Sheriff before the day was out ! That would I."

The Sheriff overheard his boast. Half in anger, and half in hope that the great brawny fellow would be able to do what he said, he made out a warrant for Robin's arrest, and handed it to Middle.

" Here is the warrant," he said. " Now go and fulfil your boast. Woe to you if you come back empty-handed ! It may be that you, in your tinker's garb, can reach the outlaw in safety—and then you must use your wits to catch him ! "

Middle was astonished and delighted. What, he, a simple tinker, bidden to go and catch Robin Hood, and given a warrant for his arrest ! Now this was greatness indeed !

He put the precious paper into his wallet, and taking his stout crab-tree staff with him, he departed in the direction of Sherwood Forest.

" I'll crack Robin Hood over the pate ! " he boasted, swinging his staff here and there. " Ay, and I'll buffet all his Merry Men too, be they never so many ! "

The day was very hot. The tinker walked for a long way, and then, being thirsty and hungry, he went to a little inn near-by. He ordered a meal, and fell to with good appetite. As he ate, he heard the host of the inn talking to a carter.

" He is a stout fellow," said the innkeeper. " No man will ever catch him, that is sure, for he has the best men in the countryside to follow him."

" Who is it you speak of ? " asked the tinker.

" Of Robin Hood," said the host. " There is a high reward out for him—but go on with your meal, Tinker ; *you* will never get it, so don't worry your head about Robin Hood ! He does not meddle with folk like you and me."

The tinker thought of the warrant in his pocket and swelled with pride.

" Ho ! " he said, rising up, " so you think no one will ever take the outlaw ? Well, we shall see. There is your money on the table, Host—and do not be surprised if next time you see me I have Robin Hood himself with me ! "

So saying, Middle walked grandly out of the inn and made his way up the hill towards the forest. Before long he met a man with merry eyes, and greeted him.

" Good-day ! " said Middle. " Have you any news of Robin Hood ? "

" Ay, plenty," said the stranger, laughing. " But why do you ask, good tinker ? "

" I have a warrant for his arrest," said Middle, slapping his wallet. " Ha ! that makes you stare ! Yes ; I, Middle the Tinker, have a warrant given to me by the Sheriff himself ! "

" Show me the warrant," said the young man.

" Not I ! " said the tinker. " Come, take my word for it, and tell me all you know of this rascally outlaw."

" Come back to the inn and let us talk there," said the stranger. " It is too hot to stand gossiping in the middle of a dusty road."

So back they went to the inn, and the young man ordered ale and wine. He told the tinker many tales of Robin Hood, at which Middle laughed uproariously. Then he began to suggest plans by which he might capture the outlaw.

Middle felt very sleepy. He had drunk a great deal of wine,

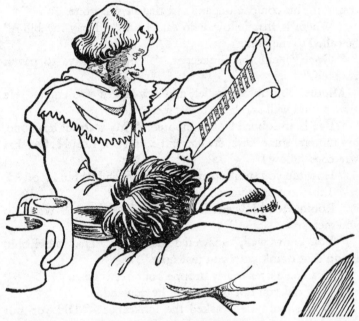

Took out the warrant and read it.

he was tired, and the sun was very hot. Before he knew what had happened, his head had fallen forward on his arms, and he was sound asleep. The stranger smiled broadly. He picked up the tinker's wallet, took out the warrant and read it. Then he put it into his own pocket, together with the rest of the things in Middle's wallet, which he left empty on the table. After that he went to the innkeeper.

"Our friend the tinker will pay the bill when he awakes," he said, with a droll wink. The host laughed and nodded. He knew his visitor well.

The stranger wondered what the tinker would do when he awoke. He hid behind a window shutter and waited to see. Soon Middle awoke and yawned widely. Then he looked round for his companion, and saw that he was gone.

"Where is that fellow who said he would pay my bill?" he called to the host.

"Gone," said the innkeeper. "You will have to pay it yourself."

Middle took up his wallet, and saw that it was empty. He gave a loud wail and leapt to his feet.

"I've been robbed!" he shouted. "My warrant has gone, my money, some keys, string, and a crust of bread! Oh that wretched fellow!"

"How can you speak so evilly of your friend Robin Hood?" asked the host in pretended surprise.

"Robin Hood!" cried the tinker in amaze. "What do you mean?"

"You know well," answered the host. "That was Robin Hood that drank with you just now."

The tinker's eyes nearly dropped out of his head.

"Why did you not tell me?" he demanded.

"Why should I?" asked the innkeeper. "Did you not say, when you departed from here the first time, that I was not to be surprised if you returned with Robin Hood? Now, pay me the score."

The poor tinker had nothing with which to pay the bill, so he had to leave his hammer and his bag behind him in settlement. Then, gloomy and exceedingly angry, he set off to see if he could find Robin Hood again.

Not more than half a mile away he saw him, walking under the trees.

" Ho, there! Stop! Stop!" he shouted at the top of his voice.

Robin turned round, and pretended to be surprised to see the tinker.

" Why, here is good Middle, who wished to find Robin Hood! Did you find him, honest tinker?"

The tinker's eyes nearly dropped out of his head.

" Ho!" gasped Middle, out of breath. " Look to yourself now, robber!"

He swung his crab-tree staff at Robin, who at once drew his sword. Then began a right good fight. Robin thought to break the tinker's cudgel with his well-tempered sword, but he could not, and Middle got in many a shrewd blow. Neither one nor the other could win the battle, and at last, panting and smarting, Robin called a halt.

But Middle would not stop. So Robin waited his chance, and then blew three blasts loudly on his horn.

The tinker flew at him in fury, knowing that the Merry Men would soon come running up; but Robin held his own, and when his men came round him, he flung down his sword and laughed. His men seized the tinker and pinned his arms down to his sides, despite all his struggles.

" Has this rascal plagued you, Master ? " asked Little John. " Shall I have a bout with him, and belabour him well ? "

" No ; let him be," said Robin. " He has a good quarrel with me, for I stole a warrant for my arrest out of his wallet."

" Yes, and also my money and my keys, some string and some bread," said the tinker fiercely.

" 'Twas but a joke," said Robin. " Here are your silver pennies, Tinker—and see, they are now changed into gold ! And here is my hand too, for you are a good fellow and a sturdy fighter."

Middle gaped to see Robin's hand held out to him. Then he put his own brawny one into it and gripped it heartily.

" Do you want a tinker ? " he asked. " Yes, surely you and the Merry Men need a tinker ? I'll mend your pots and pans, and sharpen your swords. Make me your tinker, Robin Hood."

" Shall we have him, men ? " asked Robin, looking round at all his followers, who were laughing at the tinker.

" Yes, that we will ! " cried every one, and each man came and clapped Middle on his back until he choked and spluttered and could say no word for himself at all.

Then he took the oath of loyalty, and off he went with the Merry Men, bubbling over with mirth and gladness to think that he, who had come out that day with a warrant for Robin's arrest, should now be one of his trusted men !

How King Richard came to the Greenwood

KING Richard Lion-Heart had heard so many tales of brave Robin Hood that he greatly desired to see him. Some of the stories had been against Robin, but many had been in his favour, and the King wished to find out the truth.

One day he set forth, attended by his nobles and a strong bodyguard of soldiers. When he arrived at Nottingham he went to stay at the castle there, and for many days he was feasted and entertained royally. He listened to tales of Robin Hood, and so merry and droll were they that he longed to meet the outlaw.

Therefore he wandered in the forest, hoping to see him. He and his nobles rode through the Greenwood from end to end, and yet they could not seem to meet Robin anywhere, nor did they catch a glimpse of the Merry Men.

" This is strange," said the King. " Is the outlaw still in his haunt ? "

" Yes," answered a lord near by. " I met an abbot only yesterday, who complained bitterly because he had been stopped and robbed by Robin and his men. And the day before that a knight rode into Nottingham fuming because his saddle-bags full of gold had been taken."

" Then we must try our fortune again," said the King. " To-day we will ride forth once more, and I will take only a few men with me. Perhaps too large a force frightens the outlaw."

So the King rode forth again into the forest, and went slowly through it, hoping to see Robin Hood come leaping out to stop him. But never a sign of the merry outlaw did he spy, and in great disappointment he returned home once more.

At dinner that day he found himself sitting next to the fat Bishop of Hereford, who recounted to him how Robin had dared to stop the wedding of the Lady Christabel with the old knight, and had married her to Allen-a-Dale. The Bishop was still very angry about it, but the King could not help smiling when he heard how Friar Tuck had worn the priest's fine robe, and had called the banns seven times lest three should not be enough.

" It is a strange thing that though I roam throughout the forest day after day, I can never find a trace of this bold robber," said the King. " Never once have I set eyes on him, nor he on me."

But here the King was wrong. Robin Hood knew perfectly well that Richard Lion-Heart was in Nottingham, and roamed the forest through. Robin was loyal, and loved the King, as did all the Merry Men, and he would never have harmed so much as a hair of his head.

" If the King comes our way, see that you hide yourselves, and are not seen of him," said Robin to his men. " No harm shall come to him through us. Watch also, and see that if he goes through dangerous parts there shall always be a party of you following him, for fear of wicked men attacking him in lonely glades."

" We will ! " cried all the men, and faithfully they obeyed their leader's commands. As soon as the King was sighted in the forest, they hid themselves away, and did not go near him. But if he wandered into far, lonely parts, a score or more followed behind, unseen, ready to rescue him if he should be attacked by robbers.

It was no wonder, therefore, that the King could never meet

Robin and his company, but neither he nor the Bishop of Hereford guessed why.

"My lord," said the Bishop, "can it be that you really *wish* to meet this hateful robber?"

"Yes," answered the King. "I have a mind to see if all the tales told of him are true."

"Then I can tell you how you may meet him as soon as you please," said the Bishop.

"Speak on," said the King.

"Dress yourself as a rich abbot," said the Bishop, "and take with you six men dressed as monks. Carry behind you asses laden with bags which might contain riches. Go through the forest slowly, and without doubt you will soon meet with Robin Hood and all his men. But, my lord, it is a dangerous thing to do, for I tell you that the outlaw is a wicked, fierce man, and spares no one."

The King laughed.

"It is a good plan of yours, Lord Bishop," he said. "I will try it."

So the next day he called six of his nobles to him, and bade them dress themselves in grey cloaks and hoods, so that they might pass for monks. Himself he disguised in a fine rich cloak of sober colour, and on his head he wore a tall hood that hid his face.

So dressed, the seven men called for their horses and mounted them. Behind them trotted a line of asses, laden with bags that might have contained gold, jewels, plate, or fine cloths. It was indeed a rich-looking procession that set forth to go to Sherwood Forest that day. Surely Robin Hood would show himself now!

The seven riders cantered into the forest, looking to right and left, seeking for the outlaw—and then, as they came to the thicker part of the wood, Robin himself stepped forth, his bow in his hand.

"*It is a good plan of yours, Lord Bishop,*" *he said.*

He laid his hand on the bridle of the first horse, and stopped the King.

"Not so fast, my Lord Abbot," he said. "I would have a word with you."

"Who are you?" asked the King.

"Robin Hood of Sherwood," answered the outlaw. "And you, my lord, are a rich abbot, taking your gold to the monastery. That much I can see. You must leave some of it with me."

"Wherefore?" asked the King.

"Because you rich abbots take from the poor, who can ill afford it," said Robin. "I take from the rich, and give back to the poor what you have stolen."

"Now these are bold words," said the King. "Hands off my bridle, Robin Hood!" For answer Robin blew three blasts on his horn, and out from the trees came running a score and more of his Merry Men. They surrounded the horses, and with bent bows prevented any of the King's men from getting away.

"Do you not know that I am on the King's own business?" asked the pretended abbot. "See, here is his ring on my finger. You know the sign thereon?"

Robin glanced at the ring, and knew it to be the King's. In a trice he stepped back and bowed.

"If you are the King's messenger you will come to no harm from Robin Hood and his Merry Men," he said. "We love King Richard, and are loyal to him in everything. Cursèd be all traitors to him, say I!"

"Then you curse yourself," said the King. "For you are traitors, you and your men."

"Now, if you were any other but the King's own man, I would slay you for those words!" cried Robin fiercely. "I am no traitor. I am loyal and faithful, and I would never harm the King. Have I not sent my men all these days to follow His Majesty, and see that he comes to no harm in these woods?"

Then the King understood why he had not seen Robin and his men before, and his heart warmed to the bold outlaw.

" You say you are no traitor," he said, " and yet you kill and eat the King's deer."

" Only to feed my brave men," said Robin hotly. " They must eat, my Lord Abbot, and if Richard himself could see what fine men I have, he would not begrudge his deer to them."

" Perhaps not," said Richard, with a smile. " But the King has heard many evil stories of you, Robin ; how that you rob and ill-treat travellers through Sherwood, and show no respect for Sheriff, Bishop, abbot, or monk."

"That is true," said Robin. " Who would respect robbers such as they ? Do they not take from all the peasant folk around, and oppress those for whom they should care ? The greater part of the money I take from these rogues goes back to the poor folk from whom it came, my lord."

All Robin's men listened as he spoke earnestly to the abbot, and shouted in agreement when he finished.

Robin silenced them with a wave of his hand, and then turned courteously to the King again.

" Lord Abbot," he said, " come with me, and I will dine you well to-day and give you of my best, because you are the King's man."

Richard would much rather have returned to Nottingham, where a fine feast awaited him at the castle, for he felt sure that it would be but poor fare the outlaw could offer him. But he wished to see more of Robin, so he consented to follow him and dine in Sherwood Forest.

He and his six lords were taken through the trees to the open space, beneath a large oak tree, where Robin always met his men. Here on the grass was laid what looked like a great picnic-feast. Plates, dishes, and mugs were set out on snowy cloths spread on the grass, and a fine smell of cooking rose in the air. The King was hungry, and his eyes sparkled to see the meal.

Fish there was, and fowl; fine venison from the King's own deer, and wheaten bread; wine and good brown ale—a feast fit for a king indeed!

Seven men came up and took the King's horse and those of his nobles. Then Richard and his men were led to the places of honour by Robin. Presently some little page-boys, clad in Lincoln green, ran up with basins of water for the guests to wash their hands in. The King was amazed to see how fine everything was.

When the feast was ready, Robin blew his horn. Up came a hundred and ten of his men, marching in a row. They were all clad in Lincoln green, and carried bows of good yew wood. At their sides hung short swords that glittered in the sun. When they came before Robin, each strong, sturdy man bent his knee to him before taking his place at the feast.

The King watched in surprise.

"This is a gallant thing," he thought, "and a seemly sight to see. These men honour their master as if he were their King. Would that my men honoured me as much!"

When every man was in his place Friar Tuck said grace. Then the feast began. The hungry men fell to with good appetite, and the King ate as much as any, for never before had he enjoyed a meal so much. The sky was blue through the trees overhead, the wind was fresh and sweet, and the company as jolly as ever he had looked upon. What jokes there were and what loud laughter! Richard Lion-Heart envied the outlaw his free life and his fine men.

"Is not the King's deer tasty meat?" said Robin slyly to the abbot. "Would he not forgive me if he could see my trusty men around me, feasting with right good will?"

"Mayhap," answered the King, laughing, wondering greatly what Robin would say if he knew that he really was the King.

Then Robin leapt to his feet, with a mug of brown ale in his hand.

"Up, men!" he cried. "Drink a toast to our good King, Richard Lion-Heart!"

All the men sprang up at once, and filled their mugs afresh.

"God save the King!" they cried, and drank his health with cheers. The King himself had to rise to his feet and drink his own health, for if he had not Robin would have guessed his secret.

"Now we will show our visitors what skill we have with our bows and arrows!" cried Robin. "Set up the wands and the garland of roses, Little John!"

Then far away between the trees slender willow wands were set up. Over one was hung a garland of roses, and the men had to shoot at this and get their arrows right through the flowery ring.

"The targets are too far away," thought the King. "No archer could hit so slender a mark at such a distance."

But he was wrong. Robin's men shot well, and with such marvellously true aim that every wand was split in twain. Then standing even farther away, they shot their arrows at the rose garland.

If a man failed to get his arrow through the circle, he had to give up his good yew bow to Robin, and receive a buffet on the head from Little John. So every one was careful to aim well, for no one wished to feel Little John's heavy hand.

One by one the arrows flew through the circle of roses. Then Middle the Tinker needs must have a try—but he had not had so much practice as the others, and his arrow flew wide. He pulled a droll face, and gave up his bow to Robin. Then Little John dealt him such a buffet that he fell to the ground and rolled over and over.

The Merry Men laughed loudly, for everything that Middle did was funny. The King laughed too until his sides ached, and he called upon the tinker to cease pulling such droll faces.

Then the men showed the King their fine wrestling, and also fought with staffs that he might see their skill. Richard looked on in amaze, for never had he seen such men as these. Even his own archers, the best of his court, could not hope to better these men.

Everything that Middle did was funny.

"My Lord Abbot," said Robin, at the end of the games, "will you tell the King all that you have seen? Tell him of my fine men, and how loyal they are to him. Tell him how we feasted you to-day, and treated you well, because you come from the King himself. Beg him to pardon me for killing his deer."

The King listened in silence.

"If I tell the King all this, and procure from him your pardon, would you be willing to leave your wild life in the

Greenwood, and go to serve him?" he asked. "He needs men such as you—strong, faithful, and loyal."

"Ho, men!" cried Robin loudly; "hear you what my Lord Abbot says? Would you be willing to leave this life, and go to serve the King, Richard Lion-Heart, if he will grant us all a free pardon?"

"Ay!" cried every man. They flung off their hoods, and standing bareheaded in the sunshine, they swore to serve the King as best they might.

"See you, my lord," said Robin, with pride; "we are the King's own men, faithful and true!"

The King could keep his secret no longer. He threw back his abbot's hood, and stood out before them all, tall and handsome—the King!

"I am your King, your sovereign King!" he said.

There was a great silence for a few seconds. Then Robin fell upon his knees, and all the Merry Men did likewise.

"Rise up, Robin," commanded Richard. "I give you your pardon, and all your men too. You are my friends, and no man shall call you outlaws after this. Nowhere in my kingdom shall I find men such as you!"

Then Robin rose up, and all the men too. They threw their bows into the air, and cheered wildly, vowing to follow Richard wherever he went.

"To Nottingham we will go!" cried the King. "Come, my men, follow me, as you swore to do just now!"

Then the whole troop went off to Nottingham, shouting and cheering all the way, the King riding at the head. The people of the town heard them long before they came in sight, and wondered what the excitement was. When they saw such a large company of men, clad in the famous Lincoln green, they did not know what to think.

"Have they slain the King?" said one.

"Are they coming to kill us?" cried another.

"They will take the Sheriff and hang him!" cried a third.

More and more excited grew the townsfolk. Butchers and bakers left their shops and ran to see what was happening. Men and women flung open windows and peered out. Children ran to welcome the outlaws, and cheered as wildly as they.

"Here's the King, the King himself!" shouted

"Rise up, Robin," commanded Richard.

the people, as they saw Richard at the head of the Merry Men. "What has happened? Has he pardoned Robin Hood?"

"He has pardoned Robin Hood!" ran the rumour from one end of the town to the other. Then the ploughman left his plough in the field, the smith ran from his shop, and soon every one surrounded the men in Lincoln green, and cried out to know what had happened. The Sheriff looked from his window, and stared in astonishment to see the King riding beside Robin Hood.

What excitement there was! Robin Hood had always been a favourite with the people, and now that he was pardoned by the King, they were wild with delight. The whole town made holiday, and there was merry-making all day long. Only two people did not join in the gladness—and they were the angry Sheriff and the fat Bishop of Hereford.

The next day Robin and his men went to London with the King. He was made a noble peer, Robert, Earl of Huntingdon, and Richard swore that never had any king owned such a fine bodyguard as he!

More and more excited grew the townsfolk.

The Death of Robin Hood

AT FIRST Robin was very happy in London. He loved the King, and delighted to serve him. Half of his men were with him, and the other half had been sent back to Sherwood Forest as King's Foresters and guarded the King's deer well for him. They also kept the forest free from wicked robbers.

For some time Robin Hood stayed with Richard Lion-Heart. Then the King went over the sea on another of his crusades, and left his brother John to rule in his stead. Robin disliked John, for he was mean and crafty, and oppressed the people as much as the rich abbots did in Nottingham.

For his part, John hated Robin Hood. Robin was too merry, too kindly and chivalrous for the mean-tempered prince. Soon the one-time outlaw was very unhappy, for he could not live in peace with one whose vices so far outweighed his virtues.

He began to cast his mind back to the old days when he had been so happy in the forest with all his Merry Men. He thought of the sunshine between the trees, the singing of the birds in the early morning, the laughter of his men, and the twang of the yew bows as the arrows sped away. He longed to be back in the Greenwood with all his merry company.

Then there came a sad day for Robin, for he heard that King Richard was dead, and would never come back again to his own land. Prince John became ruler, and Robin grew afraid. He felt certain that John would arrest him and throw him into prison as soon as he found an excuse. To Robin imprisonment meant something worse than death; he resolved to fly back to Sherwood, taking with him the men he had at the court.

When he told them what he planned to do, they were filled with joy. Every man had loved the old days, and the thought of roaming Sherwood Forest once more, with bold Robin Hood as their master, made them rejoice.

" No longer shall I be Robert, Earl of Huntingdon, but plain Robin Hood ! " said Robin, with a laugh. " Now, men, get ready, for at the end of this week we return to the Greenwood ! "

King John heard of Robin's resolve, and tried to stop him from fleeing away. But he was too late—Robin had just departed, and on swift horses he and his men were speeding northwards.

How glad they were to see the forest again ! How they shouted to see the glades they knew so well ! Even the birds seemed to sing more sweetly, to welcome them.

" Here did we take the Bishop of Hereford," said Robin, with a laugh, stopping on the road that ran through the forest. " And yonder is the spot where I changed clothes with the butcher long ago ! Ho, men, is this not better than London Town ? "

The men rode fast through the forest, and made their way to the open space where Robin had been used to meet his Merry Men in the old days. How his heart leapt at the sight of the great oak tree overshadowing it !

" What will the rest of the company say when they know we are here ? " cried the outlaw. " They think us still in London. Shall I blow my horn, men ? "

" Ay ! " they shouted, looking eagerly through the trees for any sign of Little John, Much the Miller's Son, Middle the Tinker, and the others. So Robin raised his horn to his lips, and once again, winding through the forest, went the old familiar sound. Three times did Robin blow upon his horn, and then paused.

Far away among the trees were the King's Foresters, the rest of Robin's company of Merry Men. They had greatly missed him, and often did they talk of the merry days of old. Little John, especially, thought always of Robin, whom he had loved with all his heart.

Suddenly the sound of a horn came through the forest. Every man raised his head and listened intently. The sound came again, and the men gazed at one another, each striving to see if the others thought the same as he. Little John stood as if he had been turned to stone, and so fearful was he lest he should lose the faintest sound of the horn, that he drew no breath for a full minute.

For the third time the high sweet sound stole through the forest, and then came no more. The men caught hold of each other's arms in excitement and wonder.

" Is it—can it be—Robin Hood ? " they said.

" That is Robin's horn ! " cried Little John, in a joyful voice, and he set off at full speed towards the sound.

" If it is indeed he, he will be under the great oak tree where we used to meet," panted Much the Miller's Son.

Never did men run so fast. Through the Greenwood they sped as if wolves were at their heels. Not a man but had the same thought in his mind—Robin Hood, Robin Hood, Robin Hood!

At last, panting and breathless, they came to the great open space where the oak tree stood ; and there, in his old place beneath the spreading branches, stood Robin, full of eagerness and pride. Little John reached him first, and flung his great arms round his master's shoulders, giving him such a bearlike hug that Robin lost all his breath.

Then each man in turn clasped his hand in Robin's, and gave his master warm welcome. Once more the Merry Men were complete, and eagerly they all talked to one another, relating adventures and telling tales. Little John would not leave Robin's side, and listened in silence to his master's words, as Robin told how he had been forced to fly from London. At the end he wanted to know only one thing.

" Master," he said, " shall we live our old free life again, with you as our leader ? "

" Yes," said Robin, and with that Little John was well content.

So once more Robin and his men became outlaws, and again they lived a merry life, feasting on the King's deer, and following their old customs. Robin's heart was full of joy to be in the Greenwood again, and he could never have enough of the company of his Merry Men. He soon forgot all about his time in London, though he never ceased to grieve for the death of his royal friend, King Richard Lion-Heart.

Now Prince John was angry because Robin Hood was living his old life as an outlaw again, defying his wishes and commands. He resolved to send soldiers into Nottingham, and order them to search the forest through, till they came upon the outlaws, and then they were to set upon them and slay them all.

A large force of archers rode to Nottingham, and made their way into the Greenwood. Robin and his men were ready for them, but would not fight until they were made to, for they did not wish to harm any brave English archer. But the captain urged on his men, and soon showers of arrows fell among Robin's company.

Then there was naught to do but to sally forth and fight. Fiercely the outlaws fitted arrows to their bows, and sent them flying among their enemy. The fight was fast and furious, and neither side would give way. When the arrows were all spent, staffs and swords were brought into play, and many hard blows were given and taken. Men on each side were slain or wounded, and it was a sad day for Robin.

All day long the two sides fought, and the peaceful Greenwood rang with shouts and groans. The birds ceased their singing and fled away. The rabbits trembled underground. The sun drew near its setting, and sent its golden rays slanting through the trees—but still the fight went on.

Not until each side was wearied to death and could fight no more did the battle stop. Then the archers and the outlaws lay down exhausted, and neither party had the strength to move so much as an arm throughout that night. When morning came the archers departed back to London, unable to fight any more, and the Merry Men, no longer very merry, looked at one another sadly, for many of their number were hurt, and some were dead.

The fight was fast and furious.

Robin himself was wounded. Little John tended him, and the wound began to heal ; but Robin seemed to have lost his strength. A fever set in, and do what he would, he could not recover from his weakness. Little John was anxious, for never in his life had Robin ailed before. He kept by his master's side day and night, and sighed to see him grow thinner and paler.

At last he grew so weak that he could hardly sit on his horse's back.

" Little John," he said, " I shall never get better unless I am tended by one skilled in medicine. I have a cousin, the Prioress of Kirkley Abbey, who will help me. You shall take me there and I will ask her to heal me. Get me my horse now, and we will go."

So Little John fetched Robin's horse, and saddled him. He lifted his master on to his back, and then, taking the bridle, he led Robin out of the forest down the highway to the nearby Abbey where dwelt the Prioress who was cousin to Robin Hood. Slowly and carefully he led the horse, but soon he saw that he would have to hold Robin on its back, for he had not even the strength to sit upright.

Half-way to the Abbey Robin fell forward on his horse's neck, and Little John knew that he would never get him to the Abbey on horseback. Gently he lifted his master down, and taking him in his strong arms he carried him the rest of the way, his heart aching to see Robin so weak.

At last they reached the Abbey, and Little John knocked at the gate. The Prioress opened it and peered out.

" Who is there ? " she asked.

" It is I, Robin Hood," said Robin. " I am ill, cousin, and would have you tend me."

" Bring him in," said the Prioress to Little John. So Robin was carried within the gates, and the Prioress led him to a small room looking out towards the Greenwood.

" Lay him down on the bed and I will bleed him," she said. " Now you must go, Little John, and leave him here to me. He must be alone, or he will not get better."

" Let me stay," pleaded Little John. " I will neither speak nor move, lady."

" No," said the Prioress. " Go back to the Greenwood, and I will send for you when you may come."

So Little John, with a last sad look at Robin, turned and went back to Sherwood Forest. He sat himself down beneath a tree, and waited patiently until he should hear that he might return to Robin.

Now the Prioress hated Robin Hood. He had taken much gold from the rich abbots and bishops who were her friends, and she longed to be revenged upon him. He was now in her power, and she could do what she would with him.

In those days, when a person was ill, it was the custom to bleed them, because the letting of blood was thought to be good for a patient. But when a little blood had run away, the wound made was always well bound up and the bleeding stopped. The Prioress meant to bleed Robin, and she set about her work.

She cut his wrist and the blood flowed. Then she pretended to bind the wound up firmly, but really she left the bandage so loose that the bleeding still went on. Robin was weary and exhausted, and paid no attention, for he thought that the Prioress was his friend. When she left him, he fell asleep.

He awoke some hours later, and felt very weak. He saw the blood still flowing, and knew that he had been betrayed. His end was near, for he was alone with no one to help him.

He tried to rise from his bed and get to the window to leap down, but he had no strength. The door was locked, so there was no escape that way. Robin groaned. How could he take leave of Little John, his true and loyal friend?

His hand fell upon his trusty horn, hanging at his side. In a trice he had put it to his lips. With all his feeble might he blew upon it—but what a faint sound came from the horn! Surely no human ear would hear it!

Little John was still sitting under the tree, waiting for news of his master. Suddenly, stealing faintly across the fields that lay between the forest and the Abbey came a thin, high sound, so feeble that Little John could hardly hear it. But he knew what it was.

"Robin! My master!" he cried, leaping to his feet. "You

D

need me, but alas, I fear you must be near dead, you blow so wearily!"

With great strides he ran all the way to the Abbey. The gates were locked, and the Prioress would not heed his loud knocking. But Little John could not be kept out. He planted his great foot against the gates, and, using it as a battering-ram, he forced them apart. He ran through and came to another

She pretended to bind the wound up firmly.

locked door. He burst this open likewise, and at last came to the little room to which he had carried Robin. One heave of his shoulder broke the door in, and he ran to where his master lay on the bed, as white as death itself.

" Ah, treachery, treachery!" groaned Little John, as he saw what the Prioress had done. " Master, grant me a last boon, I pray you."

" What is that?" asked Robin.

" Grant that I may fetch the Merry Men and burn down this Abbey, and all that are therein."

"Nay, now, Little John," said Robin; "I will not grant that boon. I never hurt woman in all my life, nor yet man that was in woman's company."

Little John knelt down by his master, and could not hide the tears that ran down his cheeks. Robin felt them on his hand, and tried to sit up.

"Raise me up, friend," he said. "Give me my good bow, and I will draw it for the last time. Where my arrow falls, there bury me. Do not grieve for me overmuch, for I have been happy, and must die some time."

Little John carried Robin to the window, and held him whilst he shot his last arrow. It flew across the fields to the Greenwood, and fell beneath an oak tree.

"Was it a good shot, Little John?" he asked.

"It was a fine shot, Master," said Little John, weeping bitterly. "Never fear, Robin; I will bury you where it fell."

"Put my bow beside me too," said Robin, and Little John promised.

So died Robin Hood. Little John faithfully kept his promise and buried him beneath the Greenwood Tree, whilst his men stood round mourning their dearly loved master; and all England was sad too when the news was known, for there were many who had loved and admired the brave outlaw. But though Robin himself passed away, his name lived on, and still in story and song we tell his fame.

Little John put a stone over Robin's grave, and on it were written these words:

"Beneath this stone lies Robin Hood,
No archer ever was so good,
Such outlaws as he and his men
Will England never see again."

The Enchanted Sword

THERE ONCE lived a King called Uther Pendragon, who loved the fair Igraine of Cornwall. She did not return his love, and Uther fell ill with grief.

As he lay on his bed, Merlin the Magician appeared before him.

" I know what sorrow is in your heart," he said to the King. " If you will promise what I ask, I will, by my magic art, give you Igraine for your wife."

" I will grant you all you ask," said Uther. " What do you wish ? "

"As soon as you and Igraine have a baby son, will you give him to me ? " asked Merlin. " Nothing but good shall come to the child, I promise you."

" So be it," said the King. " Give me Igraine for wife, and you shall have my first son."

It came to pass as Merlin promised. The fair Igraine became Uther Pendragon's wife, and made him very happy. One night a baby son was born to her and the King, and Uther looked upon the child's face, and was grieved when he rembered his promise to Merlin.

He named the tiny boy Arthur, and then commanded that he should be taken down to the postern gate, wrapped in a cloth of gold.

" At the gate you will see an old man. Give the child to him," said the King to two of his knights. The knights did as they were commanded, and delivered the baby to Merlin, who was waiting at the postern gate.

The magician took the child to a good knight called Sir Ector, and the knight's wife welcomed the baby, and tended him lovingly, bringing him up as if he were her own dear son.

Not very long after this King Uther fell ill and died. Then many mighty lords wished to be king, and fought one another, so that the kingdom was divided against itself, and could not stand against any foe.

There came a day when Merlin the Magician rode to the Archbishop of Canterbury, and bade him command all the great lords of the land to come to London by Christmas, and worship in the church there.

"Then shall you know who is to be King of this country," said Merlin, "for a great marvel shall be shown you."

So the Archbishop sent for all the lords and knights, commanding them to come to the church in London by Christmas, and they obeyed.

When the people came out of church, a cry of wonder was heard—for there, in the churchyard, was a great stone, and in the middle of it was an anvil of steel a foot high. In the anvil was thrust a beautiful sword, and round it, written in letters of gold upon the stone, were these words :

"*Whoso pulleth out this sword from this stone and anvil is rightwise king born of all England.*"

Lords and knights pressed round the sword and marvelled to see it thrust into the stone, for neither sword nor stone had been there when they went into the church.

Then many men caught hold of the sword and tried to pull it forth, but could not. Try as they would, they could not move it an inch. It was held fast, and not even the strongest knight there could draw it forth.

"The man is not here that shall be king of this realm," said the Archbishop. "Set ten men to guard the stone day and night. Then, when New Year's Day is come, we will hold a tournament, and the bravest and strongest in the kingdom shall joust one with another. Mayhap by that time there shall come the one who will draw forth the sword, and be hailed as king of this fair land."

Now, when New Year's Day came, many lords and knights rode to the fields to take part in the tournament. With them went the good knight Sir Ector, to whom Merlin had given the baby Arthur some years before.

Sir Ector had brought up the boy with his own son, Sir Kay, and had taught him all the arts of knighthood, so that he grew up brave and courteous. He loved Sir Ector and his wife, and called them Father and Mother, for he thought that they were truly his parents. Sir Kay he thought was his brother, and he was glad and proud that Kay, who had been made knight only a few months before, should be going to joust at the tournament.

Sir Ector, Sir Kay, and Arthur set off to go to the lists. On the way there Sir Kay found that his sword, which he had unbuckled the night before, had been left at the house. He had forgotten it!

"I pray you, Arthur, ride back to the house and fetch me my sword," he said to the boy beside him.

"Willingly!" answered Arthur, and turning his horse's head round, he rode swiftly back to fetch Kay's sword. But when he got to the house, he found the door locked, for all the women had gone to see the tournament.

Then Arthur was angry and dismayed, for he knew how disappointed his brother would be if he returned without his sword.

" I will ride to the churchyard, and take the sword from the stone there," he said to himself. " My brother Kay shall not be without a sword this day ! "

So when he came to the churchyard Arthur leapt off his horse, and tied it to a post. Then he went to ask the men who guarded the sword if he might take it. But they were not there, for they, too, had gone to the tournament.

Then the boy ran to the stone, and took hold of the handle of the sword. He pulled at it fiercely, and lo and behold ! it came forth from the steel anvil, and shone brightly in the sunshine.

Arthur leapt on to his horse once again, and rode to Kay.

" Here is a sword for you, brother," he said.

Sir Kay took the beautiful weapon, and looked at it in amaze, for he knew at once that it was the sword from the stone. He ran to his father and showed it to him.

" Where did you get it ? " asked Sir Ector, in astonishment and awe.

" My brother Arthur brought it to me," answered Sir Kay.

" Sir, I will tell you all," said Arthur, fearing that he had done wrong. " When I went back for Kay's sword I found the door locked. So, lest my brother should be without a weapon this day, I rode to the churchyard and took the sword from the great stone there."

" Then you must be King of this land," said Sir Ector, " for so say the letters around the anvil. Come with me to the churchyard, and you shall put the sword in the stone again and I will see you draw it forth."

The three rode to the church, and Arthur thrust the sword into the anvil, then drew it forth again easily and lightly.

Lo and Behold! the sword came forth from the anvil.

Then he put it back, and Sir Ector strove to draw it forth and could not. After him Sir Kay tried, but he could not so much as stir it an inch.

Then once again Arthur pulled it forth, and at that both Sir Ector and Sir Kay fell down upon their knees before him.

"Why do you kneel to me?" asked the boy. "My father and my brother, why is this?"

"Nay, nay," said Sir Ector. "We are not your father and your brother. Long years ago the magician Merlin brought you to us as a baby, and we took you and nursed you, not knowing who you were."

Then Arthur began to weep, for he was sad to hear that the man and woman he loved so much were not his parents, and that Kay was not his brother. But Sir Ector comforted him, and took him to the Archbishop, bidding him tell how he had drawn forth the enchanted sword.

Then once again Arthur was bidden to ride to the church-yard, this time accompanied by all the lords and knights. He thrust the sword into the stone, and then pulled it forth. At that many lords came round the stone, shouting that what a mere boy could do could be done by a man with ease.

But when they tried to draw forth the sword, they could not. Each man had his turn, and failed. Then, before all the watching people, Arthur lightly drew out the sword, and flourished it round his head.

"We will have Arthur for our King!" shouted the people. "Let us crown him! He is our King, and we will have none other!"

Then they all knelt before him, and begged the Archbishop to annoint him as king.

So, when the right time came, Arthur was crowned, and swore to be a true king, and to rule with justice all the days of his life.

The Round Table

AFTER ARTHUR had been made King, many of his lords would not come to do him homage, and made war against him. The King fought bravely against them, and soon the kingdom was his from north to south, from east to west.

Then he set about making the country safe for honest men to live in. He captured robbers, slew wild beasts, and made wide paths through the gloomy forests so that men might journey here and there in peace and safety.

There was a king called Leodegrance whom Arthur helped greatly. This king had a fair daughter, Guinevere, and Arthur loved her as soon as he saw her. He sent to Leodegrance and asked him for his daughter's hand, which that king was pleased to grant.

Then in great pomp and ceremony the two were wed, and the lovely Guinevere became Arthur's queen. Leodegrance sent Arthur a wonderful wedding present—the famous Round Table.

This had been made for King Uther Pendragon by Merlin the Magician. When Uther died, the table went to King

Leodegrance, and he in his turn sent it to Arthur, who was full of joy to receive it.

It was a very large table, for it would seat one hundred and fifty knights. Leodegrance sent Arthur a hundred knights, and the King called Merlin to him, and bade him go forth into his kingdom and seek for fifty more true knights, worthy to sit at the Table.

Merlin set out, but he could find only twenty-eight, and these he brought back with him. Thus the table was not full, and there was always room for new knights. These were ordained at every Feast of Pentecost, and very proud were men or youths when there came for them the great day on which they sat for the first time at the Round Table.

Merlin made the seats for the knights, and as soon as a new knight had sat at the table, his name appeared in golden letters on his seat. Thus the knights always knew their places, and each man took his own.

Soon all the seats were full save only one, called the Siege Perilous, which no knight might take unless he was without any stain of sin. This was not filled until Sir Galahad came, for none dared sit there save him.

The greatest day in a knight's life was when he took upon himself the vows of true knighthood, and sat at the Round Table in the company of all the other noble knights. Then he had to swear many things.

He must promise to obey the King; to show mercy to all who asked for it; to fight for the weak; to be kind, courteous, and gentle to all; and to do only those deeds which would bring honour and glory to knighthood.

So began the famous company of the Round Table, whose names have come down to us in many a brave and marvellous adventure. Any man or woman who was distressed could come to Arthur's court, sure of finding a knight who would ride forth and right their wrongs.

The Finding of the Sword Excalibur

KING ARTHUR took horse one morning, and set out to seek adventure. As he rode through the forest, he came to a fountain, and by it was a rich tent. A knight in full armour sat near by. He was tall, and very broad and strong. Never yet had he met a man who could defeat him in battle.

King Arthur made as if he would ride by, but the knight commanded him to stop.

"No knight passes here unless he first jousts with me," said the strange knight, Sir Pellinore.

"That is a bad custom," said Arthur. "No more must you joust here, Sir Knight."

"I take my commands from no man," answered the tall knight angrily. "If you would that I forswear this custom, then you must defeat me."

"I will do so!" said the King, and forthwith Sir Pellinore mounted his horse and the two rode at one another.

They met with such a shock that both their spears were shivered to pieces on one another's shields. Then Arthur pulled out his sword.

"Nay, not so," said the knight. "We will fight once again with spears."

"I would do so, but I have no more," answered Arthur.

Then Sir Pellinore called his squire and bade him bring two more spears. Arthur chose one and he took the other. Then once again they rode at one another, and for the second time they broke their spears. Then Arthur set hand on his sword, but the knight stopped him.

"You are a passing good jouster," he said. "For the love of the high order of knighthood, let us joust once again."

The squire brought out two great spears, and each knight took one. Then they rode hard at one another, and once more Arthur's spear was broken. But Sir Pellinore hit him so hard in the middle of his shield that he brought both man and horse to earth.

Then Arthur leapt to his feet, and drew his sword.

"I will now fight you on foot, Sir Knight!" he cried, "for I have lost the honour on horseback."

So Sir Pellinore alighted, and the two set about one another with their swords. That was a great battle, and mighty were the strokes that each gave the other. Soon both were wounded, but they would not stop for that.

Then Arthur smote at Sir Pellinore just as the knight was smiting at him, and the two swords met together with a crash. Pellinore's was the heavier sword, and it broke the King's weapon into two pieces.

Arthur leapt straight at the knight, and taking him by the waist, threw him down to the ground. The knight, who was exceedingly strong, rolled over on top of the King. Then he undid Arthur's helmet, and raised his sword to smite off his head.

But at that moment Merlin the Magician appeared, and cried out in a stern voice to Sir Pellinore:

"Hold your hand, Sir Knight, for he whom you are about to kill is a greater man than you know."

"Who is he?" asked the knight.

"He is King Arthur," answered Merlin.

"Then I must kill him for fear of his great wrath," cried Pellinore. He lifted up his sword, and was about to hew off the King's head, when Merlin cast an enchantment about him. His hand fell to his side, and he sank to the ground in a deep sleep. Then Merlin bade Arthur come with him, and the King, mounting on his horse, obeyed.

"You have not slain that knight by your enchantments?"

asked Arthur anxiously. " He was a great knight, and a strong and his only fault was his discourtesy."

" He will be quite whole again in three hours," said Merlin. " He is but cast into a sleep. There is not another knight in the kingdom so big and strong as he is. If he comes to crave your pardon, grant it, for he will do you right good service."

Then Merlin took the King to a hermit, and the wise man tended Arthur's wounds, so that in three days he was ready to depart.

As they rode forth, Arthur glanced down at his side.

" I have no sword," he said. " Sir Pellinore broke mine in our battle."

" No matter," said Merlin. " You shall soon have another."

They rode on and came to a broad lake. In the midst a strange sight was to be seen; for out of the water came a hand and arm clothed in rich white silk, and in the hand was a beautiful sword that gleamed brightly.

" There is a sword for you," said Merlin. " See, it glitters yonder in the lake. Below the water is a wonderful palace, belonging to the Lady of the Lake, and it is she who has wrought this sword for you. Go, fetch it."

The King saw a little boat by the side of the lake, and he untied it, and rowed on the water. When he came to the hand, he reached out and took the sword from it. As soon as he had done so the hand and arm disappeared under the water.

Arthur rowed back to land, and then, taking the sword from its scabbard, he looked at it closely. It was very beautiful, and the King was proud to have such a noble weapon. On each side were written mystic words that Arthur did not understand.

" What mean these writings ? " he asked.

" On this side is written, ' Keep me,' and on the other, ' Throw me away,' " said Merlin. " But the time is far distant when you must throw it away. Look well at the scabbard. Do you like it or the sword the better of the two ? "

"The sword," answered the King.

"You are unwise," said Merlin. "The scabbard is worth ten of the sword, for while you have the scabbard you will never lose blood, however sorely you may be wounded. So guard the scabbard well. The sword is called Excalibur, and is the best in the world."

Arthur rode back to his court with Merlin, glad to have such a fine weapon at his side. Joyfully his knights welcomed him into their company again, and once more they sat down together at the Round Table.

Before long Sir Pellinore came to crave pardon of the King for his discourtesy. Freely Arthur forgave him, and henceforth the great knight served the King well and faithfully, doing brave deeds in his service.

Balin, the Knight of the Two Swords

KING RIENCE of North Wales once sent an insolent message to King Arthur:

"Eleven kings have I defeated, and their beards make a fringe for my mantle. There is yet a space for a twelfth, so with all speed send me yours, or I will lay waste your land from east to west."

The listening knights clapped their hands to their swords in anger, eager to slay the messenger, but the King forbade them.

"Get you gone!" he commanded the man sternly.

Now there was a knight there called Balin, he who wore two swords. He was very wrath when he heard the wicked message sent by King Rience, and he vowed to avenge the insult done to Arthur.

For eighteen months Balin had been in prison for slaying a knight of Arthur's court, and he longed to do some deed that would win him the King's favour once more. So he left the hall and went to don his armour, eager to fight against King Rience.

Whilst he was arming himself, a false lady came to the hall, and reminded the King that she had once done him a service.

"In return for the good I did you, I beg you to grant me a favour," she said.

"Speak on," said the King.

"Give me the head of the knight Balin," said the lady.

"That I cannot do with honour," answered Arthur. "I pray you, madam, ask some other thing."

But the lady would not, and departed from the hall, speaking bitterly against the King. At the door she met the knight Balin, who was returning, fully armed.

As soon as he saw her, he rode straight at her and cut off her head, for he knew her to be a witch-woman and very wicked. She had caused his mother's death, and for three years he had sought for her in vain.

Then he rode forth to go against King Rience. But when Arthur found that he had cut off the lady's head, he was very angry.

" No matter what cause for anger he had against her, he should not have done such a thing in my court," said the King. " Balin has shamed us all. Sir Lanceor, ride after him and bring him back again."

Lanceor at once armed himself, and rode after Balin. He galloped his horse hard, and when he came up to Balin he shouted loudly—for he was an insolent knight—well pleased at the thought that Balin must needs go back with him to court.

" Stay, knight ! You must stop whether you will or no, and I warrant your shield will not protect you if you turn to do battle with me ! " he cried.

" What do you wish ? " asked Balin fiercely, reining in his horse. " Would you joust with me, insolent knight ? Have a care to yourself then ! "

They rushed at one another with their spears held ready, and the two horses met with a crash. Lanceor's spear struck sideways on Balin's shield, and shivered to pieces, but Balin's spear ran right through the insolent knight's shield and slew him.

Balin looked sorrowfully at the knight, for he was sad to see a brave man fallen. He buried him, and went on his way grieving.

Soon he saw a knight riding towards him in the forest, and by the arms he bore he knew him to be his well-loved brother,

" Give me head of the Balin Balin," said the lady.

Balan. They rode eagerly to meet one another, and greeted each other with joy.

"Now am I right glad to see you," said Balan. "A man told me that you had been freed from your imprisonment, and I came to see you at the court."

"I go to revenge my lord Arthur," said Balin. "King Rience has done him an insult. Come with me, my brother, and together we will follow this adventure."

The two knights rode on side by side, and presently they met the magician Merlin.

"You ride to find King Rience," said Merlin, who knew the thoughts of all men. "Let me give you good counsel, and you shall meet with him and overcome him."

"We will do as you say," said Balin, and he and his brother followed the magician to a hiding-place in the wood, just beside a pathway.

"The king will come this way shortly with sixty knights," said Merlin.

It came to pass as the magician had said. King Rience rode by with his knights, and, when he came near, Balin and Balan rose up and attacked the company.

First they unhorsed King Rience, and struck him to the ground, where he lay wounded sorely. Then they rode at the rest of the knights, and so fiercely did the two brothers fight that soon forty of the King's men were vanquished, and the rest fled.

Then Balin returned to Rience, and would have slain him, but he begged for mercy. So his life was spared, and Balin and Balan took him to Arthur's court, and there delivered him to the King to do with as he thought best.

Then the two brothers parted, and each went on his way alone.

Balin met with strange adventures, and fought many hard battles. Then one day as he rode onward, he came to a cross, and on it, written in letters of gold, were these words:

"It is perilous for a knight to ride alone towards this castle."

As he was reading this, Balin saw an old man coming towards him, and heard him speak to him in warning.

" Balin of the Two Swords," he said, " do not pass this way. Turn back, or you will ride into great peril."

When he had finished speaking he vanished. Then Balin heard a horn blow as if some beast had been killed in the hunt, and his blood turned cold within him.

" That blast was blown for me," said the knight. " I am the beast who shall die—but I am still alive, and I will go forward as befits a brave knight."

So he rode onwards past the cross, and soon came to the castle. There he was welcomed by many fair ladies and knights who led him into the castle and feasted him royally.

Then the chief lady of the castle came to him and said :

" Sir Knight of the Two Swords, know that all knights who pass this way must joust with one nearby who guards an island. No man may pass without so doing."

" That is an unhappy custom," said Balin ; " but though my horse is weary my heart is not, and I will joust with this knight."

Then a man came up to Balin, and took his shield.

" Sir," he said, " your shield is not whole. Let me lend you mine, I pray you."

Balin agreed, and took the strange knight's shield instead of his own, which had his arms blazoned on. Then he mounted his horse and rode to where a great boat waited to take him and his charger to the island.

When he arrived at the island he met a maiden, and she spoke to him in dolorous tones.

" O Knight Balin, why have you left your own shield behind ? You have put yourself in great danger by so doing."

" That I cannot help," said Balin, " for it is too late now to turn back. I must face what lies before me, for I am a knight of Arthur's court."

Then Balin heard the sound of hoofs, and saw a knight come riding out of the castle, clad in red armour, and his horse in trappings of the same colour. When this knight saw Balin he thought that surely it must be his brother Balin, because he carried two swords—for the Red Knight was no other than Balan, who had been forced by a foe to keep the castle against all comers.

But when Balan looked upon his enemy's shield, he saw that it did not bear his brother's arms, and he therefore galloped straight at him, deeming him to be a stranger.

The two knights met with a fearful shock, and the spear of each smote the other down. They lay in a swoon upon the ground, and for some time they could not rise.

Then Balan leapt up, and went towards Balin, who arose to meet him. But Balan struck first, and his sword went right through his brother's shield, and smote his helmet. Then Balin struck back and felled his brother to the ground.

So they fought together till they had no more strength left, and each had seven great wounds. Then Balan laid himself down for a little, and Balin spoke to him.

"What knight are you?" he said. "Never till now did I meet a knight that was my match."

"My name is Balan," answered the knight. "And I am brother to the good knight Balin of the Two Swords."

"Alas, that ever I should see this day!" cried Balin, in grief and dismay, for he loved his brother better than any one else on earth. Then he fell in a faint.

Balan went to him and raised his helmet so that he might look upon his face. And when he saw that it was his own well-loved brother, he wept bitterly.

"Now when I saw your two swords I did indeed think you were my brother," he said, "but when I looked upon your shield and saw that it was not yours, I did not know you."

"A knight bade me take his in exchange for mine that was not whole," said Balin. "Great woe has he brought us this day, for we have slain one another, and the world will speak ill of us both for that!"

Then came the lady of the castle and her men. She wept to hear their tale, and when the two brothers begged her to bury them in the same grave, she promised with tears that she would do so.

So died Balin and Balan, and were buried in the same place. The lady knew Balan's name, but not Balin's, and she put above their grave how that the knight Balan was slain by his brother.

Then the next day came Merlin the Magician, and sorrowfully, in letters of gold, he wrote Balin's name there too. Then below he put the story of their deaths, that all men might know how it came to pass that the two brothers had each killed the other.

Prince Geraint and the Sparrowhawk

ONE MORNING the King and all his court went hunting. As soon as dawn came, there arose a great noise of baying hounds, of tramping feet, and thudding hoofs —the knights were getting to horse.

Queen Guinevere meant to ride with the huntsmen, but she slept late, and when she arose the sun was already high. She went with one of her ladies to a little hill from where she could see the hunt passing by.

As she waited there, Prince Geraint came riding by to greet her. He too had slept late. He was not dressed for the hunt, but was clad in a surcoat of white satin, hung with a purple scarf.

He greeted the Queen, and together they waited for the hunt to pass by. As they sat there on their horses, they saw some strangers riding near. There was a knight, fully armed, a lady with him, and behind them a misshapen, evil-faced dwarf.

"Who is yonder knight?" wondered the Queen. She

turned to her maiden, and bade her go and ask. The lady rode off, and prayed the dwarf to tell her his master's name.

" I will not tell you," answered the dwarf rudely.

" Then I will ask your master himself," said the maiden.

" You shall not ! " cried the dwarf in anger, and struck the maiden across the face with his whip. She rode back to the Queen in dismay and told her what had happened.

" This dwarf has insulted your maiden and you ! " cried Prince Geraint in rage. " I will do your errand myself ! "

He rode after the dwarf, and demanded his master's name. The ugly little creature refused to tell him, and when Geraint would have ridden to the knight himself to ask, the dwarf struck the Prince such a blow across the mouth that the blood spurted forth, and stained his scarf.

Geraint clapped his hand to his sword, thinking to have slain him, but then, seeing that he was but a poor misshapen creature, he stayed his anger. He rode swiftly back to the Queen, and told her that he would ride after the knight, demand his name, and ask for redress for the wrong done to the Queen and her maiden.

" I have no armour," he said, " but that I will perchance get at the next town. Farewell, madam. I go to ride after the churlish knight."

Geraint galloped after the knight, the lady, and the dwarf, and followed them closely all that day. Up hill and down they went, and towards evening they came to a town. They rode through the streets, and Geraint saw that all the people ran to watch them pass by, leaning out of windows to see them, and peering out of doorways.

The three travellers rode to a castle at the farther end of the town, and entered the gates, which closed behind them.

" They will ride no farther to-night," said Geraint. " I will find a lodging for myself, and buy armour so that I may challenge the knight on the morrow."

But no matter where Geraint went, people seemed too busy even to answer him questions. To his request for arms, he could only get the reply, " The Sparrowhawk, the Sparrowhawk," and this strange name seemed to be on the lips of every one.

The town was full of people, and everywhere the smiths were polishing armour and sharpening swords. But for all the wealth of arms, there were none for Geraint.

" The Sparrowhawk," answered an old man, who was busy polishing a shield when Geraint asked him for help. " Have you forgotten the Sparrowhawk ? You will get no arms in this town to-night because of the Sparrowhawk."

" Who is this Sparrowhawk ? " demanded Geraint impatiently, but no one could find time to answer him. He rode through the town, and at last, despairing of finding a lodging, came to a marble bridge that led to a half-ruined castle. On the bridge sat an old man, in rags that had once been rich clothing. He greeted Geraint courteously.

" Sir," said the Prince, " can you tell me where I may get shelter for the night ? "

" Come with me, and you shall have the best that my castle can offer," said the old man. He led Geraint to his castle, which the Prince saw had been half burnt down. He took him inside, and seated by the fire Geraint saw the old man's wife and his daughter, Enid, the fairest maiden that the Prince had ever seen. She was dressed in old and faded garments, but even these could not hide her loveliness.

" Enid," said the old man, " take the knight's horse to the stable then go into town to buy bread and meat."

Geraint did not wish the maiden to do this errand for him, but she obeyed her father, and went. Soon she came back again, and set the supper for her father and his guest. She waited on them as they ate, and Geraint thought he had never before seen such a sweet and modest maiden.

"Why is your castle ruined like this?" the knight asked the old man.

"It is because of my nephew, the knight called the Sparrowhawk," said his host. "Three years ago he burnt my castle down because I would not give him my daughter Enid for wife. I am Earl Yniol, and once all this broad earldom was mine; but now I have barely enough left of my great wealth to show kindness to strangers like yourself. The Sparrowhawk lives in the big castle yonder, and, as you saw, the whole town is in a ferment about him."

"Why is that?" asked Geraint. "I could not get arms as I rode through, for every one murmured 'The Sparrowhawk! Have you forgotten the Sparrowhawk?'"

"He holds his yearly tournament to-morrow," said the Earl. "On the field is set up a silver rod, on which is placed a silver sparrowhawk. My nephew challenges all knights to win this prize from him. Two years has he won it, and when he wins it a third time, as he will, I fear, it becomes his for always, and all men will know him as the Sparrowhawk."

"This Sparrowhawk must be the knight who this morning insulted the Queen and her maiden," said Geraint. "I will challenge him to-morrow, if only I can get some arms."

"I have arms," said Earl Yniol. "But they are old and rusty. Even so, Sir Knight, you cannot enter the lists to-morrow, for only they that have ladies to fight for, and proclaim them to be the fairest there, may enter the tournament."

"Lord Yniol," cried Geraint, "let me fight for your daughter Enid, for surely she is the fairest maiden in the land! If I win, I will marry her, and she shall be my true wife."

The Earl was proud to think that such a famous knight as Geraint should ask for his daughter's hand.

"If Enid consents, you shall have your wish," he said. "Now we must seek our beds, for to-morrow you must arise early if you would enter the tournament."

An old man was busy polishing a shield.

Next day Geraint donned the rusty armour that the Earl found for him, and rode to the lists. Yniol, his wife, and their daughter Enid went to watch the tournament, praying that the brave Prince would be the victor.

The Sparrowhawk rode proudly on to the field, whilst all the heralds blew loudly on their trumpets. He called to his lady, and pointed to the silver sparrowhawk on the rod.

" Take it, lady," he said. " It is yours, for no maiden here is fairer than you."

" Stay ! " cried Geraint, galloping up. " Here is a lovelier maiden, and for her I claim the silver sparrowhawk ! "

The surprised knight looked at Geraint, and then, seeing his old rusty armour, laughed mockingly.

" Do battle for it ! " he cried.

Then he and the Prince rode at one another with their lances in rest. So fiercely did they come together that each broke his spear. Again and again they galloped on one another, and then Geraint rode at the Sparrowhawk with such fury that he smote him from his horse, and he fell to the ground, saddle and all.

Then the two set upon one another with their swords, and the sparks flew as the hard steel met.

They fought fiercely, till Geraint raised his sword, and smote the other on the helmet. The sharp weapon cleft right through it, and cut to the bone. The Sparrowhawk dropped his sword and fell to the ground.

" I surrender," he said weakly.

"Tell me your name," demanded Geraint.

" Edyrn, son of Nudd," replied the vanquished knight. " Spare my life, I pray you."

" On this condition," said Geraint sternly. " You shall return to the Earl all that you robbed him of, and you shall go to Arthur's court, and there crave pardon for your sins."

"I will do this," promised the Sparrowhawk. "Let me go now, I beg you, for my wounds are heavy."

Geraint dragged him to his feet, and he went to have his wounds dressed. Then proudly the Prince took the silver sparrowhawk from its rod, and gave it to Enid. Bitter were the real Sparrowhawk's thoughts, as he saw Geraint place it in the hands of the maiden he would dearly love to have married.

"To-morrow, fair Enid, you shall ride with me to Arthur's court, and there we will be wed," said Geraint.

That night there was merry feasting in Earl Yniol's castle, for Edyrn, his nephew, had returned to him his wealth, and many of the townspeople had brought back to the castle treasure that had been taken three years before.

The next day the Earl brought Enid to the Prince, dressed in a lovely gown that her mother had found for her. But Geraint wanted her in her old faded dress.

"Go, I pray you, and put on the gown you wore when first I saw you," he said. "I would bring you to the Queen in that robe, and she shall dress you in garments bright as the sun for your wedding."

Enid obeyed, for she wished to wear the dress in which Geraint loved her best. Then happily they set off for Caerleon, and soon arrived at the court.

Queen Guinevere kissed the shy and lovely maiden, and with her own fair hands she dressed her for her wedding. Every one loved her, and Geraint most of all.

When they were married they lived for many months at the court, and were as happy as prince and lady could be. Soon there came riding Edyrn, the Sparrowhawk, coming to crave pardon for his evil deeds. Freely Arthur forgave him, and sent him forth to do battle for him against wicked and pestilent men.

In time he became a good and true knight, and won for himself a great name in fighting for the King.

The Further Adventures of Geraint and Enid

FOR A YEAR Geraint and Enid lived at Arthur's court. Enid was loved by all, for she was gentle and kind, and Geraint was the foremost knight in every tournament, brave, handsome, and strong.

But soon there came news to Geraint of robbers in his own land of Devon. He went to Arthur and begged leave to return to his home, to fight the robbers and put them all to flight, so that once again honest men might travel without fear.

The king gave his consent, and Geraint and Enid set forth. When he came to Devon, Geraint rode out to destroy the bands of robbers. Soon he had driven them forth, and once more his country was at peace.

But when he had done that, Geraint seemed to forget that there were such things as hunts and tournaments. He loved Enid so much that he wished always to be with her, and would never leave her side. He would not go hunting, and he would no longer ride in tournaments, so that the nobles spoke his name mockingly, and the common people called him coward.

Enid heard of this, and she was grieved, for she could not bear to think that because of her Geraint was called coward. She did not dare to tell him what she had heard, but daily she grew sadder, and at last the Prince became uneasy, not knowing the reason for her pale, unhappy face.

One summer morning Enid awoke early and gazed upon Geraint as he lay sleeping. So huge he looked, and so strong, that Enid wept to think that because of her he had become weak, and would not play the part of a man.

"Alas, alas!" she said, "how grievous it is that I should be the cause of my lord's shame! If I were a true wife to him, I should tell him all that is in my heart."

At that moment Geraint awoke, and heard her words. He thought that she was reproaching herself because she no longer loved him, and was weary of being with him. He wondered, too, if she scorned him for proving himself so poor a knight of late. He asked her nothing, but in anger he called to his squire, and ordered him to get ready his horse and Enid's palfrey.

"Put on your oldest clothes," he said to the astonished girl. "You shall ride with me into the wilderness. I will show you that I am still as brave a knight as when I fought the Sparrowhawk, and won the prize for you."

"Why do you say this?" asked Enid.

"Ask me no questions," answered Geraint sternly.

Enid went to find her meanest clothes, and remembered the old, faded dress in which Geraint had first seen and loved her. She clad herself in it, thinking that perhaps, when the Prince saw her thus gowned, he would remember too, and be gentle to her.

Soon the squire brought their horses, and they mounted.

"Ride before me," said Geraint to Enid. "And do not turn back nor speak to me, no matter what you see or hear, for I would have no speech with you this day."

So Enid rode sadly in front. Soon they came to a vast and lonely forest, and there, as she rode, Enid saw four armed men hiding some way ahead.

" See," said one ; " here comes a doleful knight. We shall find it easy to overcome him, and then we will take his arms and his lady."

Enid heard these words, and was fearful, for she did not know if Geraint would see the men. Yet she was afraid to ride back and tell him, for she thought he would be angry with her.

" Still, I would rather he stormed at me, or even killed me, than that he should be set upon and slain by these robbers," she thought.

So she waited until Geraint came up to her, and then she told him of the men ahead.

" Did I not say that you were to speak no word to me ? " said Geraint in anger. Then he rode furiously at the four robbers, who came to meet him. He used such force that his spear entered the body of the first robber, and went right through it. He did the same to the second, but the third and the fourth, seeing his great strength, turned their horses aside, and fled for their lives.

But they could not escape Geraint. He rode after them, and slew them both. Then he stripped all the dead robbers of their armour, tied it upon their horses, and knotted the bridle reins together. He gave the reins to Enid, and bade her drive the four horses in front of her.

" And speak to me again at your peril ! " he said sternly.

Enid took the reins, and went forward as she was bidden, happy that her lord was safe. After some while her ears caught the sound of hoofs, and through the trees she saw three horsemen riding. Their voices came to her clearly.

" Good fortune is ours to-day ! " said one. " See, here come four horses with armour tied upon them, and only one knight to guard them."

" And he is a coward, surely," said another. " See how he hangs his craven head ! "

Enid knew that Geraint was weary with his last fight, and she resolved to warn him, even though he might punish her for speaking. So again she waited until he came up to her, and then spoke.

" I see three men, lord," she said. " They mean to take your booty for themselves."

" I would rather be set upon by three men than have your disobedience ! " cried Geraint wrathfully. Then, seeing that the horsemen were almost upon him, he rode fiercely at the foremost and smote him straight from his horse. Then he slew the other two with mighty strokes, and dismounting, he stripped them of their armour in the same manner as before, and tied it upon the horses.

Now Enid had seven horses to drive before her, and she found her task difficult. Geraint was sad at heart to see his

E

lady labour so, but he was stubborn of temper, and said nothing. They passed out from the gloomy forest, and came to open hills and fields, where reapers were at work.

Seeing that Enid was faint with hunger, Geraint beckoned to a boy who was taking dinner to the reapers. He carried bread and meat, and gaped to see such a fine knight, with a lady driving seven horses laden with armour.

" Give the lady some of the food you carry," commanded Geraint. " She is faint."

" Gladly, Sir Knight ! " said the boy. " See, I will spread all I have before you, for I can go back to the town and fetch more for the reapers."

So he spread out the bread and meat, and watched Geraint and Enid eat. When they had finished he took up the remains, and put them into his basket, saying that he would now return to the town for fresh food.

" Do so," said Geraint, " and find a fair lodging there for myself and the lady. In return for your service, you may take a horse and armour for yourself. Choose which you will from among the seven."

The boy was beside himself with joy. He chose a horse and armour, and leapt up on his steed. Then, thinking himself already a knight, he rode off to the town.

Geraint and Enid followed. They came to an inn, in which the biggest room was set ready for them. Suddenly there arose the sound of loud voices and tramping hoofs. Then into the inn strode the lord of that country, the Earl of Doorn, with twelve of his followers.

Geraint greeted him, and he Geraint. Then they ordered the host of the inn to set out a fine meal, and all of them sat down to feast. Geraint took no notice of Enid, who sat in the farthest corner, hoping that no one would notice her. But the Earl saw her, and thought she was very lovely.

After the feast was over, he went to Enid and spoke to her.

" Why do you go with your knight ? " he asked. " He is churlish to you, and treats you shamefully. Why does he let you travel without page or maiden to wait upon you ? He is truly a discourteous knight."

" Not so," answered Enid loyally. " He is my lord, and I go willingly with him wheresoever he wishes."

" Say but the word, and I will have him slain," said the Earl. " We are many, and he is but one. Then you shall come with me, and share my fair lands and my great riches."

" No," said Enid. " That I cannot do, for I love my lord, and will not leave him."

" What if I kill him, and take you with me, whether you will or no ! " said the wicked knight.

Enid was filled with terror, for she saw that the Earl would do what he said. So she answered guilefully :

" Nay, take me not by force. Come to-morrow, for I am too weary now to ride with you. Then you shall slay my lord, and I will come with you willingly."

The Earl promised to come the next day, and rode off with his followers. Geraint flung himself down on a couch, and fell fast asleep, but Enid stayed awake, watching fearfully, dreading lest the Earl should come during the night.

When dawn was near she put ready Geraint's armour, and awoke him.

" Arm yourself, my lord," she said, " for you must save both yourself and me also."

Then she told him what the wicked Earl had said to her, and though Geraint reproached her angrily for speaking to him again, he hastily armed himself, and called for their horses. In payment for his night's lodging, he left the six horses and armour, and the host of the inn could hardly believe in his great good fortune.

They had not been gone from the inn very long when the wicked Earl of Doorn came hammering at the door with forty

In alarm Enid dismounted and ran to him.

men at his back. When he heard that Geraint had gone, he was very angry, and at once galloped down the road that the Prince had taken.

Soon Enid's quick ears caught the sound of pursuing hoofs, and she turned.

" My lord," she cried to Geraint, " do you not see the Earl and his men riding down upon us ? "

" Yes, I see them," replied Geraint in wrath ; " and I see also that you will never obey me ! "

The Prince turned his horse, and rode straight at the Earl. So violently did he meet him that his foe was flung right off his horse, and lay on the ground as if dead. Then Geraint rode at the men behind, unhorsed many, and wounded others so badly that the rest fled in fear, terrified at their master's overthrow.

Seeing that his enemies were all slain or fled, Geraint signed to Enid to ride on. For about an hour they travelled forward in the hot summer sun. Then suddenly, without warning, Geraint pitched forward on his horse, and fell heavily to the ground. He had received a sore wound in his last fight, and it had bled under his armour. The knight had fainted, and now lay prone in the highway.

In alarm Enid dismounted and ran to him. She loosened his armour and tried to stop the wound with her veil. She took his head on her lap, and, leaning over him, sheltered him from the burning sun, for she was not strong enough to drag him into the shade.

Presently a troop of horsemen came that way, with the Earl Limours at their head.

The Earl stopped and looked at Enid as she sat weeping.

" Is your knight slain ? " he asked. " Do not weep for him, fair lady, but come with me, and I will treat you well."

" He is not dead ! " said Enid, weeping still more bitterly. " Oh, Sir Knight, help me to take him to some place of shelter, where I may tend him well."

"He is surely dead," said the Earl. "But for the sake of your fair face, I will carry him up to my castle."

Two servants picked Geraint up. Enid mounted her palfrey, and the troop moved off once more. Soon they reached the Earl's castle. Geraint was placed on a couch, and Enid knelt by him, trying to bring him back to life by all the means in her power.

And soon Geraint recovered a little, for he was not dead. But he still lay in a kind of swoon, hearing what passed around him, but thinking it to be part of a dream.

The Earl commanded a feast to be set ready, for he was hungry. Presently the table was spread with foods of all kinds, and the Earl and his men sat down to the meal. After a while the Earl remembered the fair lady whose knight he had brought to the castle, and he looked round for her.

"Leave your dead knight!" he called. "Come and sit by me, and you shall be my lady!"

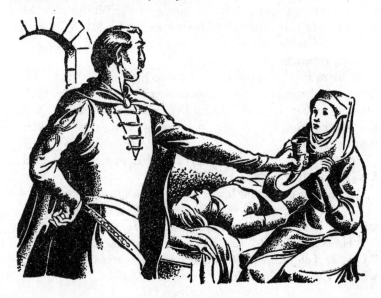

"I will neither eat nor drink till my lord eats with me," said Enid.

"You speak rashly," said Earl Limours. "You shall obey me, and drink."

He filled a goblet with wine, and went to where poor Enid crouched in terror.

"Drink!" he commanded.

"Be pitiful!" begged Enid. "Leave me to my sick lord."

Then the Earl, full of rage, struck her across the face with his hand. Enid, thinking that her lord must indeed be dead, or the Earl would never dare to do such a cruel thing, gave a loud and grievous cry.

The sound awoke Geraint from his swoon, and with sudden strength he leapt from his couch. He threw himself upon the Earl Limours, and with one blow cut his head clean off. All the rest of the people fled screaming from the hall, for they thought that a dead man had come to life.

Then Geraint turned to Enid, and looked with love and sorrow upon her.

"I had thought that you did not love me," he said, "but I did you great wrong, and I crave your pardon."

They kissed one another, but Enid was full of fear lest the Earl's men should return.

"Let us fly while there is yet time, my lord," she begged. "Your charger is outside. Let us go quickly."

She took Geraint to where his horse stood by the gate, and he mounted it, with Enid set behind him. Then together they rode off to Geraint's castle, happy once again.

And never more did Geraint doubt his lady, nor did Enid have cause to sigh that men spoke mockingly of her lord—for Geraint was ever foremost in hunt, battle, and tournament, and all men spoke his name with love and honour.

Gareth, the Knight of the Kitchen

IT WAS Arthur's custom at the Feast of Pentecost not to sit down to meat until he had seen some strange sight. There came a year when he held the feast at Kin-Kena-donne, and before he went to eat he looked about for some strange thing.

Then Sir Gawaine glanced through a window, and saw three men on horseback, and a dwarf afoot. The men alighted, and one of them was higher than the others by a foot and a half. They walked towards the King's hall, and the tall young man leaned heavily on the shoulders of the others as if he would hide his great stature and strength.

He was very handsome, and very broad of shoulder. His hands were fair and large, and very strong. When he saw King Arthur sitting on his throne he went up to him, and stood up straight and tall.

"King Arthur," said the youth, "God bless you and all your fair fellowship of the Round Table. I am come hither to ask three boons of you. The first I will ask now, and the second and third a year hence."

"Ask, and you shall have your wish," said Arthur, liking the youth greatly.

"Grant that I may have food and drink for a twelve-month," said the youth.

"Ask something better," said Arthur. "You may have it for the asking."

"I want nothing more," said the youth.

"So be it," said the King. "You shall have the food and drink you want. Now tell me your name."

"I cannot tell you that," said the youth.

"That is strange!" said Arthur. "You are the goodliest young man that ever I saw, and yet you cannot tell your name! Ho, Sir Kay! Where is Sir Kay, my steward? Bid him see that this youth has good food and drink, and is treated like a lord's son, for I like his looks very well."

"Like a lord's son!" said the churlish Sir Kay. "That were folly indeed! If he had been of high birth, then would he have asked for a horse and armour, and not for food and drink. He is a common serving-boy, and none other! He shall live in the kitchen with the other serving-lads, and eat with them.

And since he cannot tell his name, I will give him one. He shall be called Fairhands, for never did I see a serving-boy with such white hands as his ! "

Sir Gawaine and Sir Lancelot were angry at Sir Kay's mockery, and bade him cease his jibes. But Sir Kay took no heed of them.

" Come with me to the kitchen, Fairhands ! " he commanded. " There shall you have fat broth every day, and in a year's time you will be as fat as a pork-hog ! "

The youth went to the kitchen, and sat with the kitchen-lads, who jeered at him. But when they saw his angry strength, they grew afraid. Only Sir Kay mocked at him openly, and gave him the worst and the dirtiest work to do.

Fairhands did not complain, but did as he was bid. Sir Gawaine and Sir Lancelot would have had him come to their rooms for meat and drink, but he would not. He stayed with the kitchen-lads, ate with them, and slept on the kitchen floor with them at night.

But whenever there was any jousting among the knights, Fairhands was there, looking on eagerly ; and when there were games of skill between the kitchen-boys, he always beat the rest with ease ; and often Sir Lancelot would look at him, and wonder who and what he was.

At last the year was up, and the Feast of Pentecost came again. As the King was sitting at meat, there came a damsel into the hall, asking to speak with him.

" Sir," she said, " I am the Lady Lynette, and I come to your court for help."

" What is your trouble ? " asked the King.

" I come to beg your help on behalf of a great lady," said the damsel. " She is besieged in her castle by a tyrant knight, who will not let her go forth. Will you send one of your noble knights to rescue her ? "

" What is the lady's name ? " asked the King. " Where does she dwell, and who is the knight that besieges her ? "

He stood before King Arthur straight and tall.

"The wicked knight is called the Red Knight of the Red Lands," answered the damsel. "As for the lady's name, that may I not tell you."

"None of my knights can go with you if you cannot tell the lady's name, nor where she dwells," said Arthur.

But as he spoke, Fairhands came forward and stood before the King.

"Sir King," he said, "I have been for twelve months in your kitchen, and I thank you for my food and drink. Now I crave leave to ask my two further boons."

"Speak on," said Arthur.

"Sir," said the youth, "I pray you to let me have the adventure of this damsel. My second boon is that you will let Sir Lancelot ride after me and make me knight, if he thinks I am worthy."

"Your boons are granted," said the King.

But the damsel was very angry when she heard that Fairhands was to be her knight.

"Fie, fie!" she cried. "Am I to have none but a kitchen-page?"

She ran to horse and mounted in rage. Then she rode away swiftly, but Fairhands saw the way she went.

At that moment a messenger came to the youth, and told him that his horse and armour had come for him. At that every one was astonished, and went to see what manner or arms the kitchen-boy had. Outside they saw a dwarf, and with him he had a goodly horse and a fine suit of armour.

Then Fairhands armed himself quickly, and when he came into the hall to bid the King farewell, there was hardly a knight there that looked as noble as he. He took leave of the King, and then rode swiftly to join the damsel.

Every one looked after him, and Sir Kay was angry to think that his kitchen-boy was gone.

"I will ride after him and see if he knows his kitchen-master!" he cried. So he leapt to horse, and rode up to Fairhands, crying to him to stop.

"Do you know me, your master?" he said.

Fairhands turned and saw him.

"Yes, I know you well," he answered. "You are the most ungentle knight of all the court!"

With that he rode straight at Sir Kay and unhorsed him, giving him a sore wound as he did so. Sir Kay fell to the ground and lay as if he were dead. Then up rode Sir Lancelot, and Fairhands called upon him to joust with him.

So the two rode at one another fiercely, and met with such a shock that each fell to earth. Then they fought together with swords, and Sir Lancelot marvelled at the youth, for he was so big and strong that he fought more like a giant than a man. At last Sir Lancelot began to feel that Fairhands might press him too hard, and he cried out to him:

"Fairhands, do not fight so hard, for we have no quarrel, as you know. We are but jousting."

"That is true," said Fairhands. "But, my lord, it is good to feel my strength against yours. Tell me, am I worthy yet to be made knight?"

"You are right worthy," said Sir Lancelot. "Kneel before me, and tell me your name, and I will knight you here and now."

"Keep my secret, I pray you," said Fairhands, kneeling down. "My name is Gareth, and I am a son of King Lot of Orkney. Sir Gawaine is my brother."

"I am glad of that," said Sir Lancelot. "I guessed that you were of princely birth."

Then he knighted Gareth, and bade him keep well the order of knighthood. Sir Gareth rose up, mounted his horse, and with a heart full of gladness rode after the damsel.

Sir Gareth Goes Adventuring

WHEN THE Lady Lynette saw him coming, she turned to him angrily.

"Why do you come after me?" she said. "You smell of the kitchen! You are but a serving-lad and a dish-washer!"

"Say what you will," said Gareth. "I go with you, for so I have promised King Arthur, and I must follow this adventure to the end."

Now as they rode, a man came running out from the trees, and sped to Gareth's side.

"Lord, lord, help me!" he cried. "My master has been captured by six thieves, and they have bound him. I fear he will be slain."

"Take me to him," commanded Gareth.

He followed the man, and soon came to where the six robbers were. Gareth rode straight into them, struck the first one dead, and then the second. Then he turned upon the third and slew him also. The others fled, but Gareth rode after them and smote them down. Then he returned to the bound knight and unloosed him.

"I give you great thanks," said the knight. "Now as night is coming fast, I pray you bring your lady to my castle hard by, and you shall sup with me and rest there till the morrow."

So Lynette and Gareth went to the castle, and there the knight commanded food and drink to be brought. But when he would have set the damsel and Gareth together at the table with him, Lynette was angry.

"Fie on you for a discourteous knight!" she said. "Would you have us sit at table with a kitchen-boy that smells of grease? He knows better how to kill a pig than to eat with a lady!"

Then the knight of the castle was ashamed to hear her unkind words. He bade his servants set a table apart, and to it he took Gareth and sat with him, talking merrily all the night through. But as for Lynette, she supped alone.

The next day Gareth and Lynette set out once more. Soon they came to a river, and there was but one place where it might be crossed. On the other side of the ford sat two knights, and they would let no one pass over the river.

"You had better turn back, kitchen-boy," said Lynette. "You are no match for two knights."

"If they were six I should still ride onward," answered Gareth. He rushed into the water, and one of the knights came to meet him. They broke their spears, and then drew their swords. Gareth smote the knight upon his head, and he fell into the water and was drowned.

Then Gareth spurred his horse up the bank on the farther side, where the second knight awaited him. Fiercely he fought him, and it was not long before he had cleft the other's helmet, and slain him straightly.

But Lynette had no word of praise.

"Alas!" she said, "that two good knights should take their

death from the hands of a common serving-lad! You did not fight fairly. The horse of the first knight stumbled, and threw him into the water, and you went behind the second knight and struck him a false blow."

"Say what you will, damsel, I follow this adventure," said Gareth.

Then on they rode again until they came to a black and desolate land. In front of them they saw a black hawthorn tree, and on it hung a black banner and a black shield. By it stood a black spear and a black horse, and on a black stone there sat a knight, armed all in black harness, who was the Knight of the Black Lands.

"Run whilst there is time!" said Lynette to Gareth mockingly. "See, here before us is a knight who will slay you with ease."

"Damsel," said the Black Knight, greeting her, "is this knight your champion?"

"Nay; he is not a knight," said Lynette. "He is but a common serving-boy from King Arthur's kitchen."

"Then I will not fight him," said the Black Knight. "I will take his horse and harness from him, and make him go afoot. It were shame to fight a poor kitchen-boy."

"You speak freely of my horse and harness," said Gareth wrathfully. "You must fight me for them before you get them! Look to yourself now!"

With that he rode headlong at the Black Knight, and the two horses met with a sound like thunder. The Black Knight's spear broke and they drew swords. They hacked at one another fiercely, and each gave the other sore wounds. But after an hour and a half the Black Knight fell from his horse in a swoon and so died.

Then Gareth stripped the knight of his fine black harness, and took it for himself, for it was better than his own. Then he mounted the knight's horse, and rode after the damsel.

But still she would have none of him, and pushed him away from her, holding her nose daintily.

"Away, kitchen-knight, away!" she cried. "The smell of your clothes comes to me on the wind, and they smell strong of the kitchen. Alas, that such a fine knight should be slain by you! Soon you will meet one that shall punish you well, so I bid you flee away whilst yet there is time."

"I may be beaten or slain," said Gareth, "but I will never flee away."

As they rode on another knight came towards them. He was all in green, both his horse and his harness. He rode up to the damsel and greeted her.

"Is that my brother, the Black Knight, who is with you?" he asked.

"Nay, nay," she answered; "this is but a kitchen knave, who has falsely slain your brother, and taken his horse and armour."

"Ah, traitor!" cried the Green Knight, turning fiercely on Gareth. "You shall die for slaying my brother!"

"I defy you!" said Gareth. "I did not slay your brother shamefully, but in a fair fight."

Then they rode at one another, and both their spears broke. They drew their swords and began to fight furiously. Gareth's horse swerved into the Green Knight's horse, so that it fell, whereupon the knight slid lightly off, and attacked Gareth on foot. The youth at once leapt off his horse, and fought on foot also.

Suddenly the Green Knight smote such a mighty blow upon Gareth's shield that it cleft it right asunder. Then was Gareth ashamed, and he in turn gave him a buffet upon the helm. So fierce a blow it was that the knight fell to the ground, and straightway begged for mercy.

"I will spare your life only if my damsel asks me," said Gareth, resolved to make Lynette crave something from him.

"False kitchen-page, I will never beg anything from you!" said Lynette.

"Then he shall die," said Gareth, and unlaced the Green Knight's helm as if he would have slain him.

"Nay, spare me!" pleaded the Green Knight in fear. "If you will grant me my life, I and my thirty men will be yours, and will follow you gladly, for you are a fierce and lusty fighter."

"Shame that a kitchen-boy should have you and your thirty good men for his followers!" cried Lynette in a rage.

"Damsel, speak a word for me," begged the Green Knight.

"Unless the lady prays me to spare your life, you shall die," said Gareth, and he raised his sword.

"Let be," said Lynette hastily. "You miserable kitchen-knave, let be."

"Damsel, I obey you," said Gareth, and he lowered his sword. "Sir Knight, I give you your life at this lady's request. Rise up."

Then the Green Knight kneeled himself at Gareth's feet and did him homage.

"Come to my castle, where I can do you honour," he said. "You shall feast with me, and rest there for the night."

So Lynette and Gareth followed him to his castle. But the damsel ever reproached Gareth, and would not sit at table with him. So the Green Knight took him to a table apart, and sat with him gladly.

"You do wrong, maiden, to reproach this noble knight in such manner," said he. "He is no kitchen-boy, but a fair and courteous knight."

Then for the first time Lynette was ashamed of the harsh words she spoke, for she knew well that Gareth had behaved in a true and knightly manner, and had never once answered her reproaches with angry words.

She turned to Gareth and begged forgiveness.

"Pardon me, I pray you, for all I have said or done to you," she said.

"With all my heart I pardon you," said Gareth. "It gladdens me to hear you speak pleasant words, and now there is no knight living that is too strong for me, so happy am I in your pleasure."

When morning came, Gareth and Lynette set forth once more, riding together happily for the first time. They rode through a fair forest, and came to a plain on which was set a beautiful castle.

As they rode towards it Gareth saw a strange and dreadful sight, for upon great trees hung goodly armed knights, their shields about their necks. Gareth counted forty, and with a sad countenance he turned to Lynette and asked her how all the knights had met their death.

"Well may you look sad," said the damsel. "These forty knights are they that came to rescue my sister, Dame Lyonors. The Knight of the Red Lands, who now besieges the castle,

Gareth blew the horn loudly.

defeated each one, and put them to the shameful death you see. Now haste you away whilst there is time, for the knight will treat you in the same manner."

But Gareth had no thought of turning back. He rode onwards with Lynette, and soon they came to the castle.

By it stood a great sycamore tree, and on a branch was hung a mighty horn of elephant's tusk.

" Any knight that comes hither to rescue my sister, Dame Lyonors, must blow this horn, and then the Knight of the Red Lands makes him ready for battle," said Lynette.

Gareth spurred his horse eagerly, and rode up to the tree. He blew the horn so loudly that the sound echoed for miles around.

The Red Knight of the Red Lands armed himself hastily, and rode out to meet Gareth. He was harnessed all in blood red, and he rode a red horse and carried a red spear.

" Yonder is your deadly enemy," said the damsel, turning pale. " And see, yonder too is my lovely sister, the Lady Lyonors, looking down on us from the castle."

Gareth looked up to see the lady, and as soon as he saw her sweet face, he felt his heart warm with love.

" She is the fairest lady ever I looked upon," he said. " She shall be my love, and for her will I gladly fight."

Then the Red Knight called out in a loud voice :

" Cease your looking, Sir Knight, for she is my lady."

" That is a lie," said Gareth. " If she were your lady, I should not have come to rescue her from you. She loves you not. She shall be my lady, so make you ready to do battle for her."

Then the two rode at each other, with their spears in rest, and came together with such a mighty shock that both fell to the ground and lay there stunned. Those that looked on thought that each had broken his neck. But in a short time, the two knights leapt up, put their shields before them, and ran against one another with their swords.

Then began a terrible battle, and soon each knight was sorely wounded, but neither would give in. For hours they hacked at one another, and then, when each was panting for breath, they lay down to rest.

Once again they ran together, hurtling forward as if they had been two rams. In places their armour was all hewn off, and their wounds bled sorely.

So the battle went on, until Gareth, glancing up to the castle, saw the Lady Lyonors smiling down upon him with love in her eyes. Then he leapt to the fight with greater strength.

Suddenly the Red Knight struck him such a mighty blow that Gareth's sword flew from his hand, and he fell to earth. The Red Knight fell on top of him and held him down, striving to deal the death-blow.

Then loudly cried the maiden Lynette :

" Oh, kitchen-knight, where is your courage ? My sister weeps to see you so."

Her words stirred Gareth's heart, and with a great effort he rose up, leapt to his sword, and then turned once more upon the Red Knight. This time he struck his foe's sword from his hand, and when he saw the Red Knight lying on the ground, he leapt on him, and began to unlace his helm to slay him.

" I yield me, I yield me ! " cried the knight in a loud voice.

" You do not deserve your life," said Gareth sternly, " for you have put many good knights to a shameful death."

" I yield me to your mercy ! " cried the Red Knight again.

" I will release you on one condition," said Gareth at last. " You must go to the castle, and crave pardon of the Lady Lyonors for all your wrongdoing. If she forgives you, you may go free. After that you must go to King Arthur's court, and there humbly recite your evil deeds, and crave pardon of him too."

The Red Knight promised to do this, and Gareth freed him. When the Lady Lynette saw that the fight was over she hastened to Gareth and dressed his wounds. Then she had him carried into the castle, where the Lady Lyonors tended him lovingly.

Soon Gareth had won her promise to marry him, and when he returned to Arthur's court, she went with him to be wed. Then was King Arthur glad to know that the one-time kitchen-boy was no other than Prince Gareth, his own nephew. Proudly he listened to the many tales that his knights told him of Gareth's prowess and bravery.

Then the Lady Lyonors and Sir Gareth were wed with great pomp and honour, and happily did they live together at Arthur's court. As for the damsel Lynette, she came again to the court, and married Sir Gaheris, Gareth's younger brother. Then were they all happy, and lived at peace one with another

The Bold Sir Peredur

THERE WAS once a great Earl who had seven sons. Six of them went to tournaments with him, but the seventh was too young. Then one day there came news that the Earl and his six strong sons had all been killed.

The poor mother was filled with grief. She had only one boy left now—Peredur, the youngest. She took him away to a lonely place, where dwelt only women and old men, and where he would never hear of knights and tournaments, arms and battle.

Peredur grew up straight and strong. He was happy among the hills and woods, and knew nothing of the world of knights and lords. Then one day Sir Owain, one of Arthur's own knights, came riding by. Peredur saw him, and stood still in the greatest amazement. What was this fine stranger, sitting grandly on a horse more beautiful than Peredur had ever seen before ?

Sir Owain reined in his steed, and spoke to the boy.

" Have you seen a knight pass by this way ? " he asked.

" A knight ? " said Peredur. " I pray you, tell me what a knight may be."

" One like myself ! " said Sir Owain, laughing.

Then Peredur felt the saddle with his strong fingers.

" What is this ? " he asked, and the knight told him. Then the youth took hold of Sir Owain's sword and spear, and asked their names too, and what they were used for. The knight told him all he wanted to know, and then Peredur bade him farewell and ran off.

He went to where the horses were kept—gaunt, bony creatures used for carrying firewood—and picked the strongest out for himself. He placed a pack on the horse's back for a saddle, and then picked some supple twigs from which to make himself trappings such as he had seen upon Sir Owain's steed.

Then he went to say farewell to his mother, for he had resolved to be a knight like the man he had spoken to. The poor woman was full of distress, but she did not keep him back. Instead, she gave him some good advice.

" Ride to Arthur's court," she said, " for there you will find the noblest company of knights in the kingdom."

Peredur proudly rode off. He was a queer figure on his bony old horse. He held a long, sharp-pointed stick in his hand for a spear, and he thought gladly of the day when he would indeed be a knight.

After many days he came to Arthur's court. At the same moment there rode up an insolent knight, so vain of his strength and skill that he was resolved to fight with any one of the King's knights and, by overthrowing him, gain glory and honour for himself.

This knight entered the hall in front of Peredur, and snatching up a goblet, threw the wine it contained straight into the face of Queen Guinevere.

" Does any knight here dare to avenge the insult I do the Queen ? " cried the arrogant knight. " If any one of you is bold enough to do battle with me, let him follow me to the meadow, where I will speedily overcome him ! "

With that he strode out, mounted horse, and rode to the

field. All the knights in the hall were dumb with amazement at the insult to the Queen, and not one moved, so much were they astonished.

But Peredur, who was just behind the stranger knight, was stirred with anger.

" I will do vengeance upon this evil fellow ! " he cried. Then he turned, and, swiftly mounting his horse, rode after the insolent knight.

But when the knight saw him coming on his bony horse, he laughed loudly. " Tell me, boy," he said, " is any knight coming to do battle with me from the court ? "

" I will do battle with you," answered Peredur fiercely.

" I will not fight with such a scullion as you ! " cried the knight in scorn. " Go back to Arthur's court, and tell the knights they are cowards, and I have shamed them all ! "

" You shall fight with *me* ! " said Peredur grimly. " You shall give me that goblet whose wine you dashed into the Queen's face, and you shall give me your horse and armour also ! "

Then in anger the knight rode at Peredur, and struck him a fierce blow in the shoulder with the butt-end of his spear.

" Would you play with me ? " said Peredur. " Then I will play too."

He rode at the insolent knight and drove his sharp-pointed stick at him. It entered his eye, and straightway the knight fell from his horse and died.

Peredur leapt down, and ran to him, eager to take his armour and his horse, so that he might be dressed like a knight. But he did not know how to undo the fastenings of the armour, and he could not drag it off, try how he would.

Then Sir Owain galloped up, hot from Arthur's court, and stopped in amaze to see the arrogant knight slain by an unskilled youth, whose only weapon was a stick.

" What are you trying to do with his armour ? " he asked.

The poor woman was full of distress.

"I want it for myself," said Peredur, "but I cannot undo the fastenings."

"Leave the dead knight his arms," said Sir Owain. "I will gladly give you my own horse and armour. But first come with me to Arthur and he will knight you, for you have proved yourself well worthy of the honour."

"I accept your gift," said Peredur, rising. "But I will not come to Arthur's court until I have proved myself in other adventures."

Sir Owain helped the youth to put his armour on, and then gave him his own fine horse. He bade the bold lad farewell, and watched him ride off to seek further adventures.

Peredur, rejoicing in his new arms and steed, rode on gaily. Many a knight he met on his way, and jousted with them. He overthrew each one, but spared every man's life, only bidding him go to Arthur's court and say that Peredur had sent him.

Then one night he arrived at a castle, and begged for food and shelter till the morning. He gained admittance, and a meal was set for him at the table of the lady who owned the castle. But sadness and gloom hung over the Countess, and the meal was poor, for two nuns brought in six loaves and a decanter of wine, and that was all the food there was.

"Pardon the poor fare," said the Countess, blushing, "but I am in great trouble."

"Tell me your distress, and I will help you," said Peredur.

"There is a wicked baron near here, who wishes to marry me," said the lady. "I refused his offer, and because of this he has taken all my lands from me, and left me only this castle. All my servants are fled, and there is no food left save the loaves and wine which some kind nuns have brought me."

"To-morrow I will do battle with this robber!" said Peredur eagerly. "I will overthrow him, and force him to return to you all those things that he has stolen."

The next day Peredur put on his armour and rode out to meet the baron. He saw a great host spread over the plain, and riding out from it a proud knight on a beautiful black charger. He was the baron, and scornfully he accepted Peredur's challenge to fight.

Fiercely the two rode at one another, and met with such force that the baron was thrown off his horse, and lay on the ground stunned. Peredur at once dismounted and, drawing his sword, he ran to his foe. He stood over the fallen man, who, as soon as he came to his senses, saw that he was about to be slain.

" Mercy, I pray you, mercy ! " he groaned.

" Mercy you shall have, but only when you earn it," said Peredur sternly. " First you must break up your army, then you must restore threefold to the Countess what you have taken from her, and last of all you must submit yourself to her as her servant."

The baron groaned again, and promised to do all that Peredur demanded. The youth let him rise, and then rode back to the castle. Here he stayed until the baron had fulfilled his promises, and then proudly he rode away.

As it chanced, Arthur's camp lay near by, for the King, hearing great tales of Peredur's prowess, had come in search of him. Sir Owain saw the youth as he stood by a stream, and rode up to ask his name. As soon as he saw it was Peredur, he welcomed him gladly, and bade him go with him to Arthur.

Peredur rode to the camp, where the King smiled upon him, and bade him take his rightful place among the brave Knights of the Round Table. Then Sir Peredur, proud and glad, rode back to the court with valiant knights for company, and with an exultant heart sat down for the first time at the Round Table. Many were the brave and bold deeds he did, and he was soon famed throughout the kingdom for his courage and his daring.

The Quest of the Holy Grail

IT HAPPENED one year at Pentecost that all the knights went to hear service in the chapel. When they came forth, each took his seat at the Round Table. Every place was filled save one, the Siege Perilous, in which no knight dare sit save only he that was without stain of sin.

That morning, as the knights went to take their places, they saw that something was written on the Siege Perilous in letters of gold. This is what they read:

"Four hundred and fifty years after the Passion of our Lord Jesus Christ shall this seat be filled."

Then all the knights were amazed, for when Sir Lancelot made a reckoning, it was found that exactly four hundred and fifty years had gone by—therefore the Siege Perilous should that day be filled.

As the knights stood marvelling, there came a squire to the King, and told him of a wondrous sight.

"Sir," said he, "floating down the river is a stone, and in it is a sword."

"I will see this marvel," said the King.

So he and all his knights went out to the river, and there they saw the stone floating. It was of red marble, and in it was thrust a fair sword, on which were written these words: "Never shall man take me hence, but only he by whose side I ought to hang, and he shall be the best knight in the world."

"Sir Lancelot, surely this sword belongs to you," said Arthur. "Take it, I pray you."

But Sir Lancelot, brave and noble knight though he was, knew well that he was not the best in the world, and he would not take the sword. Sir Gawaine tried, and Sir Percivale, but they could not move the sword from the great red stone.

Many another tried also, but not one was strong enough to take the fair weapon from its place.

"Let us return to our meat," said Arthur. "This sword belongs to none of you."

The knights left the river, and went back to the Round Table, where each took his seat. Soon all were filled save only the Siege Perilous. Then another marvel came, and every knight sat silent in wonder.

Suddenly all the doors and windows of the hall were closed by unseen hands. Then there appeared an old man, dressed all in white, and by him walked a young knight in red armour, without sword or shield, and with an empty scabbard by his side.

"Sir King," said the old man, "I bring you here a young knight of kingly descent. Through him shall many marvels be wrought."

"You be right welcome," answered the King.

Then the old man unarmed the young knight, and took him to the Siege Perilous. He lifted up the silken cloth that covered the seat, and there, instead of the words that had been seen before, were new ones.

"This is the seat of Galahad, the high prince," shone out in letters of gold.

The young knight sat down in the seat. The old man went forth, leaving him alone in the midst of the knights. They looked at Galahad in the greatest awe and wonder, for none had ever dared to sit in that place before.

"He is so young," murmured the knights among themselves. "But he is pure of heart and without sin, and his countenance is fair and truthful."

When the company arose from the table, the King took the young knight to the river, and showed him the stone in which was the sword.

Galahad put forth his hand and drew the sword from the stone lightly and easily. He slipped it into his empty scabbard, glad to have such a fair weapon. But as yet he had no shield.

Now that evening, as the knights sat again at the Round Table, they heard the rumbling of heavy thunder, so near that it seemed as if the roof were about to fall in upon them. Then, stealing into the great hall, came a sunbeam seven times brighter than any they had ever seen. In its light the knights looked upon one another, and each of them seemed fairer of face and nobler than before.

Then gliding into the sunbeam came the Holy Grail, covered with a silken cloth, so that none could see it nor who held it. Every knight was filled with happiness and awe, and gazed upon the strange sight in silence.

Suddenly it vanished. The knights drew breath again, and gave thanks to God for the good grace He had sent them.

The Holy Grail was the sacred cup out of which the Lord Jesus Christ had drunk before He died. It was sometimes seen by mortal men, but only by those who were pure of heart. The knights had not seen it completely—for it had been covered by the silken cloth.

Then Sir Gawaine sprang to his feet, and made a vow.

" I will go in search of the Holy Grail ! " he cried. " I will seek for it until I see it uncovered. If I cannot find it within a year and a day, I will return, knowing that it is not for me."

All the other knights leapt up too, and made the same holy vow ; but King Arthur was sad, for he knew that the quest would break up his brave company of the Round Table.

" Never again shall we all meet here," he said. " Some of you will die, some will be slain—only a few will return to me. The Evil days have begun."

On the morrow the King arrayed all his knights before him, and there were a hundred and fifty. Then they bade him farewell, mounted their horses, and rode away. The people of the town were sad when they went, for they were the noblest company that ever was seen. The King wept also, for never again would he see the Round Table filled with all his noble fellowship of knights.

With the knights went Sir Galahad in his red armour, the youngest of them all. His adventures we follow, for he it was who fulfilled the quest.

F

The Adventures of Sir Galahad

SIR GALAHAD rode onwards for four days without adventure. Then he came to a white Abbey, where he found another knight of the Round Table, King Bagdemagus.

"What brings you here?" asked Galahad.

"Sir," said Bagdemagus, "there is a wonderful shield here, which must only be worn by the best knight in the world. I know well that I am not the best knight, but I shall take the shield and wear it, and see what adventure befalls me."

"He who wears the shield wrongfully shall meet death or great misfortune within three days," said a monk. "Look to yourself, King Bagdemagus, for only he to whom it belongs may wear it without harm.

"I will wear it," said the King. "If aught happens to me, then Galahad shall try it next."

The next day the monk took the two knights to where the shield hung behind an altar. It was as white as snow, and in the middle was a red cross. Bagdemagus took it and slung it about his neck.

"Abide you here until you learn how I fare," he said to Galahad. Then set forth, followed by his squire.

Now he had hardly gone two miles when a knight, clad all in white armour, and seated on a white horse, came riding swiftly towards him. The King saw that he was about to fight him, and he set his spear in rest. The two galloped hard upon one another, and Bagdemagus broke his spear upon the other's shield. But the White Knight smote him so hard that his spear broke the King's armour, and went right into his shoulder. He fell from his horse, and lay still on the ground. Then the

White Knight dismounted, and took away the shield from the King.

"Your folly is great," he said. "This shield is not yours."

Then he took it to the squire, and gave it to him, saying: "Bear this shield to the good knight Sir Galahad, for it belongs to him."

"Sir," said the squire in awe, "what is your name?"

" That is not for you or any earthly man to know," said the White Knight.

So the squire took the shield to Galahad, who hung it about his neck with gladness. Then he went to fetch Bagdemagus, who lay ill of his wounds for many months, but escaped at last with his life.

Sir Galahad rode on his way until he came to an old chapel, where he knelt to pray ; and as he prayed a voice came to him that said : " Go now, adventurous knight, to the Castle of Maidens, there to do away with its wicked customs."

The knight took horse again, and rode on till he saw before him a strong castle with deep ditches. There he saw an old man, and asked him the castle's name.

" Fair sir," said the old man, " it is the Castle of Maidens. Therein live seven wicked knights who are brothers. They lie in wait for knights and their ladies. When they have killed the knights, they take their damsels, and imprison them in the castle, so that nothing but weeping and wailing is heard there day and night."

" I will do battle with these evil knights," said Galahad.

He rode on towards the castle, and suddenly out from the gates there came rushing the seven knights.

" Now you have met your death ! " they cried to Galahad.

" Are you all going to fight me at once ? " asked the knight.

" Yes ; therefore look to yourself ! " they shouted.

Galahad, undismayed, rode at the foremost knight, and smote him to earth with his spear. The second knight struck such great strokes on Galahad's shield that his spear broke. Then they drew their swords.

Galahad rode fiercely at the knights, using his sword so valiantly that he filled them with terror. They jerked their horses round, and rode away at full speed, terrified lest Galahad should pursue and kill them. But the knight let them go ; he wished to enter the castle and free the imprisoned maidens.

Taking the keys from an old monk, Galahad entered and freed all those whom the wicked knights had imprisoned. With cries of gratitude and joy the maidens flocked round the young knight and thanked him.

Then Galahad summoned all the knights of the country round about, and bade them do homage to the maiden to whom the castle belonged, and promise to serve her faithfully and well. Then the next day he set out once again on his adventures.

As he departed there came a messenger to him, telling him that the seven wicked knights had met Sir Gawaine, Sir Gareth, and Sir Owain, and had been slain by them in fair battle.

" That is good news," said Galahad. " They will return no more to this castle."

The young knight rode on, meeting many adventures. In all he proved himself a true and honourable man, and so great was his might that no knight could withstand him.

One day, as he rode, he encountered Sir Lancelot and Sir Percivale. Neither of them knew him, for his armour was strange, and they challenged him to joust with them. The knight accepted the challenge, longing to prove his strength against two such famous knights as these.

He rode at Sir Lancelot, whose spear broke on Galahad's shield. So mighty was the blow Galahad gave that Lancelot was smitten to earth with his horse. Then the young knight drew his sword, and rode at Sir Percivale. He smote him on the helmet, and the sturdy knight fell straight out of his saddle.

Then, before the two knights could find out who he was, Galahad rode away, marvelling that he had been able to hold his own so well with Lancelot and Percivale—for each was famous in jousts and tournaments, and much feared in battle.

There came a day when Galahad rode to the sea-shore. There he met a maiden, and she bade him enter a ship, saying that he should soon see the highest adventure that ever any knight saw

When the knight stepped on board, he found Sir Percivale and Sir Bors there, and they welcomed him gladly. As the ship sailed on her way, they each told their adventures, and marvelled at them.

At last they arrived at the castle of King Pelles, and he welcomed them with joy. That night the vision of the Holy Grail came to the three knights. They saw it shining under its silken covering, on a table of silver. Angels came and set candles on the table, and bade the knights come to eat the holy bread.

Tremblingly they came. Then a Voice spoke to them, bidding them take the silver table and the Holy Grail to the city of Sarras, where more marvels should be done.

" To-night the Holy Grail shall depart from this place," said the Voice, " but you must go to the sea-shore three days' ride from here, and there you will find a ship, in which you will once again see the silver table and the Holy Grail. This ship shall take you to the city of Sarras."

The listening knights obeyed the commands of the holy Voice. When the silver table and the Holy Grail vanished, they took horse, and rode for three days until they came to the sea-shore. There they found a ship, and when they went on board they saw in the middle of it the silver table, and on it the Holy Grail, covered with red samite.

Then Galahad fell upon his knees, and prayed for the day to come when he might see the Holy Grail uncovered, and might join his Lord Jesus Christ in Heaven.

Soon the ship came to the city of Sarras. The three knights landed, taking with them the silver table. But it was very heavy, and Galahad, seeing an old man sitting at the gate of the city, called to him to come and help.

" Truly," said the old man, " it is ten years since I was able to stand upright ; I cannot help you."

" Do not think of that," said Galahad. " Rise up and come."

The old man tried to stand—and to his great amazement he found that he could do so. His crooked bones became straight, and he could walk without crutches. Then joyfully he ran to the silver table, and helped the three knights to carry it.

It was not long before the whole city knew of the miracle. The King heard the wonderful story, and commanded the knights to come before him.

They obeyed, and told him of the marvellous table of silver, the Holy Grail, and the Voice that had bade them come to the city of Sarras.

But the King was a heathen, and when he heard of the God of the three knights he was angry, and gave commands that they should all be thrown into prison. For a whole year they lay there, forgotten by everyone.

Then the wicked King fell ill, and remembered the three knights. He asked for them to be brought to him, and when they came he begged their forgiveness, which they gave him.

Soon afterwards he died, and the people of Sarras did not know whom to choose for their next King. Then, as they talked one with another, there came a Voice among them.

" You shall choose the youngest knight of the three to be your King," said the Voice. The people listened in awe, and made haste to obey. They took Galahad, and crowned him, begging him to rule them, and to give them good laws.

The young knight could not refuse, for they would have slain him. He accepted the crown, and for a year he ruled Sarras wisely.

At the beginning of the second year Galahad went with Percivale and Bors to the chapel where the silver table was kept. As soon as Galahad entered he saw an old man there, surrounded by angels.

" Come hither," said the old man to Galahad. " Thou shalt now see what thou hast always longed to see."

Galahad knelt down among the angels.

Then Galahad knew that he was about to see the Holy Grail uncovered, and that the vision would be glorious beyond compare. He began to tremble, for he was afraid of such great joy. He went to Percivale and kissed him, and then to Bors, bidding each knight farewell.

Then he went to the table and knelt down among the angels. Soon, in a dazzling light, he saw the Holy Grail uncovered, and the vision was so marvellous that the young knight prayed he might ascend to Heaven at that moment. He had no wish to live longer in the world after his vision of heavenly things.

His prayer was granted, for even as he prayed his soul left his body, and was borne upwards by angels.

This was seen by Sir Percivale and Sir Bors, who saw also a Hand, which came down from Heaven and took away the Holy Grail.

When the angels had gone, and the chapel was once more empty, the two trembling knights saw that Galahad was still kneeling at the holy table. They went to him—but he was dead, for the angels had taken his soul, as they had seen.

Then they lamented, for they had loved him. They buried him with honour, and all the people of the city sorrowed. Then Sir Bores entered a hermitage, and became a monk, but Sir Percivale took ship, and went back to his own land. He rode to King Arthur's court, and there told him of Sir Galahad's marvellous vision, and of how he had died in the seeing of it.

" Now the quest of the Holy Grail is ended," said King Arthur. " The best knight in the world has seen it, and no man shall dare to say hereafter that his eyes have beheld the vision."

The King spoke truly, for since then there has never been a man hardy enough to say that he has seen the Holy Grail.

Sir Mordred's Plot

THERE WERE two knights of Arthur's court, Sir Mordred and Sir Agravaine, who hated Sir Lancelot, for he was always first in tournaments, and all men spoke well of him. The King and Queen loved and honoured him more than any other knight.

Sir Mordred was bitterly jealous, and at last the hatred he felt grew so fierce that he longed to harm Sir Lancelot and make the King think evil of him.

So he and Sir Agravaine went about saying that Lancelot and the Queen plotted treason against Arthur. Their three brothers, Sir Gawaine, Sir Gareth, and Sir Gaheris, heard these false words, and commanded Sir Mordred to cease the saying of them.

" We will tell the King himself," said Sir Mordred fiercely. At that the five brothers began to quarrel. Then the three younger ones strode away in anger, unable to make Sir Mordred and Sir Agravaine promise to hold their lying tongues.

The King heard their quarrel, and bade Sir Mordred tell him what all the noise was about.

" Sir," said Mordred, " I will keep silence no longer. Here is a thing you should know. Queen Guinevere and Sir Lancelot love one another, and because of their love they are plotting treason against you."

Arthur loved Sir Lancelot with all his heart, and he would not believe what Sir Mordred said. The wicked knight left him in rage, vowing that he would prove to the King that what he said was true.

He waited until Arthur had gone on a journey, and had left Guinevere behind. As was her custom, she sent for Lancelot to come and talk with her in the evening. He went to her, clad in a rich mantle, and unarmed. He did not dream that Sir Mordred and Sir Agravaine, with twelve other knights, were hiding near by, watching.

No sooner was Lancelot in the Queen's room, talking with her, than the fourteen knights leapt out from their hiding-place, and ran to the door.

"Traitor knight!" they cried, hammering on the door, "we know that you are plotting treason against the King! Open, and let us take you!"

The Queen and Lancelot leapt up in surprise. The knight laid his hand to where his sword should be, and groaned when he remembered that he was unarmed. What could he do against fourteen fully armed men ?

The knights outside were still shouting and hammering on the door. Then they fetched a bench, and tried to break it down. Lancelot could no longer bear the cries of " traitor " hurled at him, and he resolved to meet the knights, even if it meant his death.

He wrapped his mantle thickly round his arm, and opened the door a little way, so that but one knight could come in. This was a huge man, Sir Colgrevance, who with his sword struck at Sir Lancelot mightily. But the knight put aside the stroke and gave Sir Colgrevance such a buffet on the helmet that he fell dead to the floor.

At once Lancelot dragged the knight inside the room, shut the door again, and bolted it. Then he stripped Sir Colgrevance of his armour and donned it himself.

He flung open the door, and stood there to face the thirteen knights. At one blow he slew Sir Agravaine, and then he stepped fiercely towards the other knights. So full of wrath was he and so mighty that not one man could withstand him. One after another he slew, and at last none was left save only the wicked Sir Mordred. Him Sir Lancelot wounded sorely, so that he fled away with all his might.

Then Lancelot returned to Guinevere and begged her to ride away with him.

" If Mordred goes with his lying tongue to the King, and tells him that there was treason between you and me against Arthur, and that I have killed Sir Agravaine and twelve other knights of the Round Table, there will be heavy punishment for us both," said Lancelot. " Come with me, where you may be safe, for Arthur in his anger may condemn you to death."

But Guinevere would not go.

" I must stay here and meet the King myself," she said.

He opened the door a little way.

Meanwhile Mordred was riding swiftly to Arthur, to tell him of the night's happenings. The King was amazed to see him stagger from his horse, and come to kneel before him, wounded and bleeding.

" Sir, we have proved treason," said Sir Mordred. " Also Sir Lancelot has killed Sir Agravaine and twelve other knights of your fellowship. We demand that you condemn your false Queen to death."

Alas ! Arthur could do nothing else, for he must keep the law of the land, which said that treason was to be punished by death. He sent for Sir Gawaine, and sadly commanded him to bring out the Queen to be burnt.

" That I will never do," said Gawaine. " She is a noble lady, and you do wrong to consent to her death."

Then Arthur sent for Gawaine's younger brothers, Sir Gareth and Sir Gaheris, and bade them to bring the Queen to the burning. They were young and dared not disobey, but their hearts were very heavy.

" We will obey," said Gareth. " But it is a hard thing you have commanded us."

When the day came, the Queen was fetched to the burning, and many lords and ladies wept to see her, so pale she was and sorrowful. Only Mordred and his company were merry, for they knew that the Queen's death would mean terrible sorrow to Lancelot, the knight they so bitterly hated.

But that brave knight was not going to let Guinevere suffer death for his sake. He waited until she had been tied to the stake, and then he galloped up, scattering aside all those who were in his way. Mordred and his friends drew their swords and attacked him ; but never was there a knight who could withstand Lancelot. He laid about him with right good-will and his enemies went down before him, wounded or dead.

He hacked his way to the stake, and then cut Guinevere's bonds with his sword. He swung her up on his horse, and sword in hand, galloped away again, none daring to stop him, so terrible was his might.

But little did Lancelot know what he had done in his slaying —for he had all unawares killed both Sir Gareth and Sir Gaheris, brothers to Sir Gawaine. In the heat and the press he had not seen them, and his avenging sword had slain them among his enemies. They lay dead beside the stake.

When it was told to Arthur that the two young knights had been slain by Lancelot, he sat in great anguish of heart, for he knew that Sir Gawaine, their brother, would be overcome with grief.

When Gawaine came in, he asked for news, and it was told him that Lancelot had rescued the Queen from her burning.

" That was knightly done," said Gawaine. " But where are my two brothers ? "

" They are slain," answered the man who had brought the news.

" That cannot be," said Gawaine. " Who should slay them ? "

" Sir Lancelot slew them," said the messenger. " They lie dead beside the stake."

Then Gawaine gave a dreadful cry and ran to Arthur.

" My lord, my lord," he said, with the tears bursting from his eyes, " my two brothers are slain on Lancelot's sword."

" Take comfort, Gawaine," said the King, himself weeping with sorrow. " Lancelot killed them in the great press around him, and did not know that they were there."

" O my two fair brothers ! " said Gawaine, almost out of his senses with grief. " Never will I rest until I have avenged their deaths. Henceforth all my life I will spend in striving to slay the evil knight who slew my brothers ! "

Then King Arthur looked with unhappy eyes into the future —for he knew that his noble fellowship of the Round Table was for ever broken.

Sir Gawaine meets Sir Lancelot

SIR GAWAINE would not let King Arthur rest, but bade him take arms against Sir Lancelot, and do battle with him. So the King marched against the knight's castle, and grievous was the killing on the battlefield, and many a noble knight was slain.

Then the Pope of Rome heard that the two greatest knights of the world, King Arthur and Sir Lancelot, were at war one with another. He sent a message to each, bidding them cease.

He commanded Lancelot to return Guinevere to the King, and he bade Arthur take her back in peace and forgiveness. Each promised to obey, and when the day came for Lancelot to ride to the court with Guinevere, there was great stir among the knights and lords on both sides.

The King sat waiting in his great hall, with his knights about him. Then came Sir Lancelot riding with the Queen, and they entered the hall, and knelt before Arthur.

"I bring you your Queen," said Lancelot to the King, "and, my lord, there is no truer or more honourable lady in the land, and I will do battle with any knight who denies my words."

But none spoke, not even Gawaine, for though he hated Lancelot bitterly, he had always honoured the Queen.

The King looked sadly on Sir Lancelot, for he had loved him well.

"You were my best-loved knight," he said. "And now you have brought great sorrow upon me."

"If you speak of the slaying of Sir Gareth and of Sir Gaheris," said Sir Lancelot, "there is no man alive feels more sorrow for that than myself, for I held both knights in love and honour, and Sir Gareth was knighted by me."

The Queen and Sir Lancelot knelt before Arthur.

"You are a traitor," said Sir Gawaine fiercely, "and never will I forgive you for slaying my two fair brothers. If my lord Arthur will not fight for me, and avenge their deaths, then I will leave him, and I and my friends will do battle with you alone."

"Peace, Gawaine!" said Arthur. "Sir Lancelot, you must leave the kingdom, and see that before fifteen days are past, you and all your men are gone."

Then Lancelot looked round the hall, and was heavy of heart, for he knew that never again would he sit at the Round Table with his friends. And many there were who wept to see that noble knight depart, but none spoke him farewell.

Very soon Lancelot gathered all his kinsmen together, and departed to France, where he had great lands. But even when he was gone Gawaine could not forget the vow he had made to avenge his brothers' deaths by slaying Lancelot.

"My lord king," he said to Arthur, "I pray you take your army to France, and do battle with the traitor there. Have you forgotten already how Lancelot killed Sir Gareth and Sir Gaheris, both of whom loved him so well?"

Arthur knew that if he did not consent to Gawaine's wish, the knight would leave him, and take with him his friends and kinsmen. So few of the knights were now left that the King could not bear to lose more; therefore he agreed to take an army to France, and force Lancelot to fight, though it was sorely against his will.

"I will make Sir Mordred, my nephew, ruler of my kingdom whilst I am gone," said King Arthur. So this was done, and the false knight rejoiced in his great power. Then over the sea went Arthur and all his host.

Sir Lancelot retired into his strong castle, and let Arthur's knights waste his lands as they would, for he could not bring himself to fight against the King he loved so well. But his own knights were angry, and begged him to let them go and fight.

"I will send to make peace," said Lancelot. "I will tell the King of the love I bear him, and maybe he will listen. If he does not, then we will fight."

So Lancelot sent a fair damsel to Arthur, charging her to plead with the King, and to tell him that for love of him he would not fight. The damsel mounted her palfrey and rode to Arthur's camp.

Many knights there hoped that the King would listen to her pleadings, and declare peace, for there was not one that did not love and honour Lancelot as the noblest knight living. When she began to remind the King of the glorious days of the Round Table, of the friendship that had been between him and Lancelot, and of the many times that that great knight had saved the King from death, Arthur wept for sorrow.

Then would he fain have told the damsel that there could be no more war between him and Lancelot, but only love and honour. But Sir Gawaine would not let the King have peace, and he turned on Arthur in anger.

"You must have your way, Sir Gawaine," said Arthur sadly. "I do not forget that this quarrel is yours, because of your fair brothers, Sir Gareth and Sir Gaheris. I will send no message to Lancelot; you shall tell the damsel what you will."

"Then return to Sir Lancelot," said Gawaine to the weeping maiden, "and tell him that so long as I have life in my body I will seek to slay him. Tell him he is a traitor and a coward, and no true knight."

The damsel departed, and rode back to the castle. When the knights there heard Gawaine's message, they were very angry, and shouted for battle. But Sir Lancelot stood silent with the tears running down his cheeks, grieved to the heart to think that the goodly fellowship of the Round Table should be so broken up and divided against itself.

The next day the King's knights came riding round the castle. Sir Gawaine was with them, and he rode up to the walls and shouted for Lancelot.

"Where is that traitor knight?" he cried. "Where is he who plotted treason against my lord Arthur? O Lancelot, do you hide within your castle like a coward?"

Then Sir Lancelot knew that he must fight with Gawaine, or lose his honour among knights. He mounted upon his horse, and rode proudly out of the castle with all his men.

Gawaine rode to meet him, and when the armies saw these two powerful knights set against one another, they drew apart. It was arranged that no man should go nigh them; they should fight their battle to the end.

Sir Gawaine and Sir Lancelot galloped their horses furiously at one another, and each knight smote the other in the middle of his shield. So strong were they, and so big their spears, that the horses could not stand the shock, and both fell to earth. The knights leapt lightly off, put their shields before them, and drew their swords.

For three hours the two knights fought a hard battle, and sore were the strokes that each gave. Soon both were wounded, and the watching hosts marvelled that men so sorely hurt could fight. Sir Gawaine, fierce in his great anger, was stronger than Sir Lancelot, and many a time that great knight feared to be defeated and shamed by him.

But at the end of three hours he felt Gawaine's strength go, and knew that he would vanquish him. He doubled his strokes, and gave Gawaine such a buffet on the helmet that the knight fell to the ground and could not rise again. There was no man living that could withstand the buffets of Sir Lancelot.

The knight withdrew from Gawaine, but Gawaine cried out to him:

" Why do you go from me? Now turn again, false traitor knight, and slay me, for if you leave me thus, I will do battle with you again when I am whole."

" You know well, Sir Gawaine, that I would never smite a fallen knight," said Sir Lancelot.

Then he went to his castle; and Sir Gawaine was borne to his tent, where his grievous wounds were dressed. For many weeks he lay ill, but vowed still that he would slay Sir Lancelot —for never could Gawaine forget the death of his two brothers, Sir Gareth and Sir Gaheris.

The Passing of Arthur

Now as soon as the King was gone over the sea, the false Sir Mordred gave out that Arthur had been killed in battle. He made himself King, and sent to Queen Guinevere to say that he would wed her, and she should be his Queen.

The people believed that Arthur was dead, and welcomed Sir Mordred, promising to fight for him. But when it came to Arthur's ears that his nephew had usurped his throne, and meant to marry Guinevere, he was very wrath, and made haste to return to his kingdom.

Sir Mordred resolved not to let the King land, for he knew that if the people saw Arthur, they would know that their rightful King was not dead, and would go to fight under his standard. So he got ready a fleet of ships, and gave Arthur battle off the coast of Dover.

But the King's knights were very powerful, and Mordred could not prevent them from landing. There was a fierce battle, in which many knights were wounded, and then Mordred and his men fled away.

After the battle, King Arthur gave commands that those that were dead should be buried. Then was noble Sir Gawaine found in a great boat, dying. When Arthur heard this, he went to him, and took him into his arms, sorrowing his heart out.

" Sir Gawaine, my sister's son, here you lie, the man I love most. You and Sir Lancelot were my greatest friends, and now have I lost you both."

" Mine uncle, King Arthur," said Gawaine, " my death-day is come, for I am smitten upon the old wound that Sir Lancelot gave me. And now I see that by my haste and wilfulness I

have brought sorrow and death to full many a knight, because I would not make peace with Lancelot. If he had been with you now, your enemies would not have dared to rise against you, for the name of Lancelot is feared and honoured throughout the kingdom. Alas that I should have quarrelled with such a noble knight ! I pray you, mine uncle, set pen and paper before me, for I would write to Lancelot before I die."

Then, when pen and paper were set before him, Gawaine wrote his last letter :

"I, Gawaine, send you greeting, and would have you know that I am smitten upon the old wound you gave me, wherefore I am brought to my death-day. I beseech you, Sir Lancelot, return again to this kingdom and say a prayer for me at my tomb. Also, by all the love there was between us, do not tarry, but come over the sea in all haste, that you may with your noble knights rescue our well-loved lord, King Arthur, who is greatly pressed by his false nephew, Sir Mordred."

Then Sir Gawaine died, and the noble knight was buried with much honour and sorrow, for he had been greatly loved.

Sir Mordred fled to the west, and King Arthur pursued after him, resolved to give him battle and defeat him sorely. At last he came up with him, and planned with his knights to attack his enemy on the next day.

But that night Sir Gawaine came to Arthur in a dream, and warned him that if he fought on the morrow he would meet his death, and so would all his noble knights.

"Make a treaty with Sir Mordred," said Gawaine. "If you have truce for a month, then Sir Lancelot will come to you again with all his men, and you shall win a great victory. And you and Sir Lancelot shall hold one another in friendship again as heretofore."

Then Gawaine vanished, and the King awoke. He called his men around him, and told them his dream. Then all of them declared that they must make treaty with Mordred, and delay the battle for a month.

So the next day a message was sent to Sir Mordred, asking for a council to be held, to make a treaty ; and it was decided that each side should take fourteen knights to the meeting.

Before Arthur went to the council he called his chief knights before him.

"I in no wise trust this false traitor, Sir Mordred," he said. "He may mean treachery, though we meet in peace. If you see the flash of a sword, see you come on fiercely, for you will know you are needed."

Then Arthur and Mordred, and fourteen knights with each, went to the council ; and they agreed to make peace for a month. But as they sat at the meeting, an adder crept out of the bushes, and bit a knight on the foot.

He felt the sharp pain, and when he saw that an adder had bitten him, he drew his sword to kill it.

His weapon flashed in the sun, and both sides saw it! At once all thought that there was treachery afoot, for the watching hosts could not see the adder. Then trumpets and horns blew loudly, men shouted, and the two armies ranged themselves to fight.

"Alas, this unhappy day!" said King Arthur. He mounted his horse, and rode back to his host, while Sir Mordred did likewise.

Then began a fearful battle, and great blows were given on either side. Brave knights fell by the hundred, and many daring deeds were done. All day long the battle raged, and of all the knights there was none so brave as King Arthur himself.

When evening drew on, the King looked around him. He groaned in dismay and sorrow when he beheld, of all his noble company of knights, but two alive, and they were sorely wounded. Sir Lucan and Sir Bedivere were the knights, and they went to their lord in sorrow.

On the other side there was but one knight left, and he was Sir Mordred. The battlefield was strewn with hundreds of dead, and it was a sight to make the bravest man weep.

"Alas, that ever I should see this doleful day!" said the King. "Where are all my noble knights? Would to God I knew where that traitor Sir Mordred is, that has caused all this mischief."

As he spoke, he saw Mordred not very far distant, leaning on his sword among a great heap of dead men.

"Now give me my spear," said Arthur to Sir Lucan. "I will slay this traitor with mine own hand."

Then, with his great spear in his hand, the King ran towards Sir Mordred, crying, "Traitor! Now is thy death-day come!"

He thrust with great might through Sir Mordred's shield, and the spear entered the traitor's body, standing out behind a good way. Mordred knew that he had received his death-

There came an arm above the water and caught the sword.

stroke, and with his last remaining strength, he took hold of his sword with both hands, and brought it down upon King Arthur's helmet. Then he fell back and died.

Arthur sank to earth in a swoon, for his head had been cleft by the sword. Sir Lucan and Sir Bedivere came to him, and lifted him up to carry him to a place of shelter. But Sir Lucan's wound was so great that his brave heart burst, and he fell dead by Arthur's side.

When Arthur came to his senses, and saw Sir Lucan there, and his brother Sir Bedivere weeping by him, he could scarcely speak for sorrow.

" Sir Bedivere," he said at last, " I would have you do a thing for me. Take Excalibur, my good sword, and go with it to yonder water side. Throw it into the water, and then return to me again to tell me what you see."

Sir Bedivere took the sword and departed. But on the way to the water he looked at the beautiful weapon, and grieved to think that it should be thrown away.

So he hid Excalibur under a tree, and returned to the King, saying that he had done as he was commanded.

" What did you see when you threw the sword into the water ? " asked the King.

" Nothing but waves and wind," said the knight.

" You speak falsely," said Arthur sadly. " Go again to the water, and throw the sword in, as I bade you."

Then Sir Bedivere turned again, and fetched the sword, to do the King's bidding. But again he looked at the noble weapon, and thought it great shame to fling it away. So once more he hid it beneath a tree, and returned to Arthur.

" What did you see this time ? " asked the King.

" Nothing but the rippling of the water," answered the knight.

" Ah, traitor untrue ! " said the King. " Now you have betrayed me twice. Do as I command you, or with my own hands I will slay you, for you are no true knight to me, Sir Bedivere, if you will not do my last wish."

Then Sir Bedivere was ashamed, and taking the sword, he went with it to the water. He threw it out as far as he might. Then there came an arm above the water, and caught the sword, brandished it three times, and so vanished.

Then the knight returned to the King, and told him what he had seen, and Arthur was content. Sir Bedivere took him upon his back, and carried him to the water side; and there came by a barge with many fair ladies in it, with black hoods, crying and wailing.

"Now put me into the barge," said King Arthur, and it was done. Then the barge was rowed out from the land, leaving Sir Bedivere alone by the water side.

"Ah, my lord Arthur," cried the dismayed knight, "what shall become of me, now that you are gone, and I am alone?"

"Comfort yourself," said the King. "I go to the Island of Avalon, to heal me of my grevious wound, and if you hear of me nevermore, pray for my soul."

Then the barge passed out of sight. Sir Bedivere gave a dolorous cry, and fled into the forest weeping and wailing.

No more is written of the great King Arthur, but there are some that say he is not dead, but dwells still in the happy Island of Avalon, from whence he will come again when his kingdom needs him.

Others say that he is indeed dead, and that his tomb lies in the distant West. On it is written these words:

"HERE LIES ARTHUR, ONCE KING
AND KING TO BE."